HIS WILD ATTRACTION

A WILD BILLIONAIRE ROMANCE

WILD BILLIONAIRE ROMANCE
BOOK 4

C.D. GORRI

HIS WILD ATTRACTION

A Billionaire Romance Novel
Wild Billionaire Romance Book 4
By
C.D. Gorri
Copyright C.D. Gorri, NJ 2024

Before you begin sign up for my newsletter here:
SUBSCRIBE HERE

To all you amazing ARC readers, booktokers, and bookstagrammers who helped support me in this endeavor to take on the world of contemporary romance. Thank you so much for your support and encouragement. It means the world to me.
And for the rest of you who picked up my Wild Billionaire Romance series. I hope you enjoyed these not so sweet romance tales featuring our four possessive book boyfriends and the curvy women they obsess over. <3
Thank you so much for reading!

These wild billionaire playboys are used to getting their way…

There isn't much money can't buy, especially when it comes to pleasure. But can these curvy women tame these billionaire beasts and win their love? Or will their souls be sucked into oblivion by the wanton bliss their bodies crave more and more with every surrender?

Each of our heroes wears a mask on the outside to face the world, but his disguise comes off when he runs into the one female who makes his blood run hot. Need and possessive passion abound in these books, but our heroes know only one way to control their desires.

Will they f*ck the feeling they see as weakness out of

their systems, or will their needs only grow more wild with every touch, kiss, and plunge into ecstasy with the object of his affections?

Our Billionaire Heroes
Adrik Volkov
Marat Volkov
Josef Aziz
Andres Ramirez

Content Warnings
(I think I got it now…thank you for the feedback!)
*The FMC briefly lived at a shelter for abused women and children after her ex was violent towards her. There is discussion of physical abuse by a spouse.
*This series has profanity, graphic steamy scenes, violence, homicide, talk of deceased relatives, references to sexual assault and abuse (not by the MCs), mention of domestic violence (not perpetrated by MCs), mention of suicide, alcohol consumption, misogyny (not the MCs), questionable morals, hurtful past, manipulations, fake relationships, lies, revenge, forced marriages, very bad decisions, and romantic obsessions that may be unhealthy. This is a fictional story with fictional characters. This is not real life.
Always take care of your mental, emotional, and physical

self because you are important. If you are seeking help from a violent spouse or partner, call the National Domestic Violence Hotline at 800-799-7233.

**She needed shelter from the storm.
He just needed her.**

Ellie Maxwell was a mother trying to protect her son from an abusive ex. Befriending the *wives of wolves* wasn't something she sought, but it was something she needed.
It wasn't easy to pick yourself up after someone tried so hard to knock you down. But with these ladies' support, Ellie was on her way. That they were married to very powerful men didn't hurt, either. There was just one problem.

Andres Ramirez.

Called the *prince of acquisitions*, Andres was a rising star at Volkov Industries. His genius for business was renowned, but his penchant for making Ellie moan was a total secret. One she couldn't afford to indulge.

Andres' attraction to the sweet-looking woman was off the charts. She was constantly on his mind, plaguing his dreams with images of the one time they were together. But the woman seemed determined to ignore him.

Just when he thought he might go mad, she called with an outrageous proposition. Marry her to stop her ex? Yes. He could do that. Andres knew Ellie was it for him. This was his shot to prove it to her.

But did the laws of attraction still apply when only one of the players was wild for the other?

Six Months Ago

"Mommy? Where are we going?" Sammy's sweet voice whispered in the darkness.

"Hush, Baby. It's okay. Mommy's here. We're going somewhere safe," I whispered, and gathered my son close to my body with my one good arm.

He was scared and upset, and my heart broke for him. A child should never see a father hurt his mother.

Gary was the man who'd vowed to love and cherish me. He was the man who insisted on starting a family right away.

But somewhere deep in my mind, I must have known he wasn't a genuinely good person. Somewhere deep in my heart, I must have realized what he really wanted. And it wasn't me. Or Sammy.

Fuck.

This was all my fault. Tears pricked my eyes, whether it was from the pain in my body or the crack in my heart, I wasn't sure.

But I couldn't let Sammy see my despair, so I sucked it up, and left the midtown condo where I'd lived with my husband with our son in my arms. I had a backpack slung over my shoulder with a few things I'd hastily thrown together.

My wallet. Sammy's birth certificate. Some cash. A few articles of clothing for both of us, and our toothbrushes.

Our first stop was to the ER where a doctor treated my injuries and wrapped my broken arm in a hard cast.

I was lucky it was a clean break, and I didn't need surgery. She was sympathetic and agreed to not argue about how I'd sustained the injury for my son's sake.

Sammy was tuckered out and slept on the exam table beside me as I signed myself out of the ER.

Our second stop was at St. Elizabeth's Shelter for Women and Children. I'd seen signs for the shelter posted all over town and knew where it was located.

I never imagined I would need such a facility, but I was so tired, and I had nowhere else to go.

No family left. No friends—Gary had made sure of that. And no support system.

I never finished college, and I didn't have a job. Gary was like my father in that respect. They both had very outdated views of women.

Gary wanted his wife to stay at home and keep the house running neatly.

I didn't mind that so much.

In fact, my joy of cooking was very real. The only thing that rivaled it was being Sammy's mother. I would have been happy being a modern housewife raising our child, if only he'd loved me even a little.

Sammy was the only good thing to come of our marriage. My rambunctious boy was bright and sweet. Not that Gary was any kind of father to him.

I used to brush it off. Make excuses. He was a busy man. Older than me by almost fifteen years. Gary Peters worked for my father, and when we first met, he'd showered me with all the attention my father had denied me growing up.

My mother had died when I was young, and I was sure a therapist would have a field day diagnosing me. But I had no time for that.

No, this wasn't the first time Gary had hit me, but it was the first time he'd left bruises.

I was so fucking ashamed of myself for allowing it to get this far. But I would deal with my emotional baggage later.

Sammy came first.

Always.

He was supposed to start preschool this year, but with everything that happened, I never enrolled him.

It was probably for the best. I would never have been able to explain these bruises, or the broken arm.

Fuck Gary.

Anger filled me when I thought of that piece of trash I'd married. I took a calming breath and clutched Sammy's hand in mine. He yawned and pressed his head into my thigh, and I swallowed down my emotion.

My sweet, sleepy boy, you're okay. I'll make sure you're safe from now on. I will never be weak again.

That was my promise to my son, and I would keep it. There was nothing I wouldn't do for him.

"Hi, I'm Meredith. Welcome to St. Elizabeth's. We're so glad you're here now." A kind-looking woman with gorgeous red hair and green eyes came to meet me.

"I'm Ellie. This is Sammy," I said, and she bent down and greeted my shy son with a smile.

Sammy hid behind my leg at first, but eventually he came out of his shell, coaxed by cookies and toys.

"Want to tell me about it?" she asked when he was distracted.

"Where should I start? With how stupid I am for letting myself be a victim?" I said, my self-loathing evident.

"No. You're not stupid, Ellie. And yes, you were victimized, but that was a moment in time out of your whole life. You can choose not to be a victim. Coming here was the first step," she said, her voice rich with sympathy.

"I never thought I would end up in a place like this," I confessed, hating that I sounded weak and naïve, and maybe even a little judgmental.

"Ellie, no one expects this or plans it. At St. Elizabeth's, we believe everyone deserves to feel safe. It's our mission to help families like you and Sammy move from a place where you lacked the basic security everyone is entitled to, to a place where you can breathe freely again. Let me help you both. Please," she implored.

Meredith's big green eyes filled with compassion, and more than that, I could sense the basic goodness inside of her. She wasn't judging me, even if I was.

And she wasn't pitying me.

That was important to me.

You have no idea how important.

It'd been so long since anyone had offered to help. Longer still since I felt seen. I sucked in a shuddering breath and felt the tears pricking my eyes.

She was right.

Gary was a monster. But I wouldn't be his victim.

I couldn't allow him to have that hold over me. Not when I had Sammy to think about.

So, on that bright spring afternoon, I told my entire story to a complete stranger, and sought shelter for me and my son.

And it's the first best decision I made since leaving him.

It all started when I stepped into a pile of cat shit.

Yeah, cats used litter boxes, but only when they're clean. Some cats were pickier than others, according to the internet, and everyone knew the internet was always right.

I had a system in place. I scooped daily and changed the cat litter every eight days.

Rocky was still technically a kitten. Only nine months old, or so the animal rescue place had said. He shouldn't require more frequent cleaning than that.

It was a jumbo sized litter box, for Pete's sake!

Meredith had been kind enough to allow pets in the Morristown housing where Sammy and I recently moved. It was an offsite location from the Manhattan branch of St. Elizabeth's Shelter for Women and Children.

Sammy and I were residents there for a couple of months, but Gary had found us and started sending letters with thinly veiled threats. He showed up twice, harassing the poor employees who worked there, some of them volunteers.

I didn't want that for any of the kind people there who'd been so helpful to me. I was getting ready to leave, though I didn't know where I'd go, when Meredith offered me use of this place.

We were the first residents, and I couldn't be more grateful to her.

The friendship that had sprouted between us, and her friends Sofia and Destiny Volkov, was as unlikely as the sky turning pink, but it had happened.

Somehow, some way, those three women had gently brought Sammy and me into their group, and I was constantly amazed. I mean, I never had girl-friends like them.

Sammy was supposed to start preschool this year, he'd be four in a few months. But with everything that happened, well, I'd been too terrified about sending him where Gary could get him.

With Meredith, Sofia, and Destiny, not to mention the latter two's children, in our lives, I had to admit my shy boy was thriving. Even their husbands made an effort to speak kindly to my son, and they often bought toys and played with the children whenever we had one of our Sourdough Sunday lunches.

Funny how living in a million dollar condo in Manhattan never made him smile. But move him to a couple of small rooms in Morristown, where he could finally have a kitten of his own and, well, my boy had been smiling nonstop.

"Meow."

Grrr.

Back to Rocky. So, as I was saying, scoop daily, and change the litter every eight days. He was only eight pounds, but he was gaining weight.

Anyway, he must not have been happy with the state of his box this evening, so he found some place else to do his business.

I growled, hopping to the sink where I lifted my foot and grabbed some flushable wipes.

Apparently, Rocky, though picky about pooping in his box when his litter wasn't fresh, wasn't above dropping a deuce inside the pile of clothes I left on the bathroom floor after Sammy's bath time.

Ugh.

After I wiped the chunky part off, I scrubbed my heel with a handful of ivory and rinsed, repeating the process six times before I felt clean enough.

The good news was, the clothes were relatively unblemished, since the turds were hard and dry.

Not hard enough to withstand being squished by my fat ass when I stepped on one, but hard enough that the laundry could sit after being spritzed with stain remover until tomorrow.

Anyway, I blamed the cat shit for why I did what I did tonight.

It had to be the cat shit.

n hour prior to the cat poop incident I couldn't get him out of my head.

It was wrong.

Ridiculous.

Pathetic, even.

I thought I was done mooning over this man. This sexy as hell stranger who had more muscles than anyone needed, sexy, tribal tattoos covering his biceps, a killer mouth, and stormy bedroom eyes.

Fuck.

I should never have let him touch me.

Was he the one who touched you? My inner bitch snarked.

Shut up.

But my inner bitch was right. I was the one who jumped him.

My cheeks burned with embarrassment as I recalled that evening with perfect precision.

How good he smelled, like spicy cologne and man. How hot he looked in a pair of gray slacks and a knit polo shirt. His trimmed beard and short hair felt so soft beneath my fingers, and that mouth.

Christ, his mouth.

Swoon.

Had I ever been kissed like that before in my life?

The answer was a loud, resounding *no*.

So yeah, when Andres Ramirez had offered to drive me and Sammy back to our new place at the offsite St. E's residence in Morristown, I said yes.

Once he walked us upstairs, putting a sleeping Sammy to bed, I practically tackled him in the small living room of my new apartment.

Meredith had started this program with me and Sammy in mind. After Gary started showing up at St. Elizabeth's in Manhattan, she knew I couldn't stay there.

The house in Morristown was perfect for our needs, and I had no doubt it would benefit others who needed to switch locales.

We spent one wild night touching, kissing, and

having the kind of sex I'd only ever read about before.

The man played my body like a master. It was like Andres could read everything I was feeling on my face, and he knew exactly what I needed and how I needed it.

I flew apart in his arms, chasing the sun, and flying so high I never thought I'd come back down.

But I did, of course. No one could stand that kind of pure pleasure indefinitely. It would kill you.

I couldn't explain what made me behave so recklessly. Hell, we hadn't even used protection.

I was on the pill. And I hadn't had sex of any kind the last couple of years of my marriage to Gary.

Not that he was anything like Andres in the bedroom, or, *um*, living room, as it were.

I was clean, was my point, and I was on the pill to regulate my period. Yes, I should have asked him about his own history, but it wasn't planned, and I would deal with any unfortunate outcome on my own.

There were none—*thank goodness*—and yes, I scolded myself and picked up a box of condoms just to have. Like just in case there was a repeat, which there wouldn't be.

I'd made sure of that. Because, after our passionate interlude, I ignored him.

Like completely ignored him.

Well, what else was I supposed to do?

Andres Ramirez was out of my league. He was already taking up way too much space in my brain than any man had the right to.

A partner at Volkov Industries, the company co-owned by my new best friends' husbands, Andres was not only single, sexy, and good with kids, he was also a damn genius.

I barely finished one semester of college. But my lack of formal education wasn't the only obstacle between us.

Andres was gorgeous.

Like super freaking hot. He had stormy eyes not quite blue and not quite gray, but some sort of in between color that simmered with emotion whenever I looked at them.

He had short, dark hair, a close-cut beard, and bronzed skin covering his many muscles.

I mean, really? Who the heck had eight abs, anyway?

I was a newly divorced single mom with boobs that were slightly too small for my frame. My hips were too wide, my thighs jiggled when I walked, and my ass was too fat. I had cellulite bumps to prove it.

Flaws my ex liked to point out repeatedly during our marriage.

And let's not forget all my fucking baggage.

There was a lot of it thanks to my piece of shit ex. Gary Peters. Total fucking slimeball.

Shit.

I shuddered anytime I thought about my former husband. That gem of a man had not only hit me and threatened our son, but I just got slammed with his latest demand.

Gary was now demanding alimony and visitation rights with Sammy.

I'd named my sweet almost-four-year-old boy, Samuel Alexander Maxwell-Peters, after my grandfather.

Gary didn't protest the hyphen. Which was good, because if I got my way, I was going to dump his name entirely.

What kind of piece of shit asked his wife for alimony?

Worse, what kind of father never saw his son for more than ten minutes at a time during the almost four years the child lived with him, but was suddenly interested after the divorce?

I was so mad I could spit.

But I would give him money if it meant keeping

him away from Sammy. Only the sonofabitch wouldn't take any of the cash that was now frozen during the slew of inquiries Gary's attorneys had drawn up regarding my father's will and company.

He wanted more than money. He wanted to hurt me, yes, but more than that, he wanted control of my late father's company. That was all Gary Peters ever wanted.

Maxwell Mining was the multimillion dollar corporation my great-grandfather started over a hundred years ago.

Yeah, my family was old money.

I was the only remaining Maxell. Well, no, actually, Sammy was the last Maxwell.

God, I felt so stupid.

I knew some people experienced worse things than what I'd been through. And my heart broke for anyone who had to suffer at the hands of an abuser.

But I was so damn mad at myself.

I'd been young when I met Gary. Stupid, inexperienced, and naïve. He was older and experienced.

He'd flattered me and teased me. Made me feel special. But I knew now it was all a lie.

Gary never wanted me. And he never wanted Sammy.

He admitted to purposely getting me pregnant,

thinking it would make him the next heir to my father's business.

But my father was grossly old-fashioned. He believed men were made for business, and women were made for keeping house. I was never taught anything about the business.

Not a fucking thing. And I never cared because I didn't want to learn anything about mining.

I was a silly, sheltered little thing. I never wanted to do more than knit, and bake, and be a wife and mother.

Maybe it was because of my father's ideals. Or maybe I was just as old-fashioned. I couldn't really say.

Everyone was different, right? The world was full of people who all liked what they liked regardless of anyone else.

So what if I spent all my time reading novels and watching DIY shows, helping our cook in the kitchen, and learning to crochet from my nanny when I was growing up?

I was all for being independent and strong. But I thought that meant doing the things I liked.

I was lucky, I knew that. I didn't have to worry about money.

Even without learning the family business, I had

a trust fund. And when Gary proposed, I thought I would finally get everything I wanted.

Husband. Home. Baby.

I didn't know he was using me. And I didn't know my husband would turn vicious when he didn't get what he wanted.

My father never believed a girl could run his company. Yes, I was his sole heir, but Dad set up procedures to sell the company when he died, leaving me a fortune, of course. But that was all.

But Gary was contesting everything. My money, my inheritance, and everything having to do with the business were all tied up in court. It would be months before I saw a dime.

That left me with few options.

Goddamn him.

I couldn't believe I'd lost both my father and the rose-tinted glasses I'd viewed the world with just under two years ago.

My father had been sixty when I was born. He was much older than any of my school friends' parents.

Maybe I should have expected it, but his passing from a sudden stroke still hurt.

My father wasn't a cruel man. He just had

different ideas about what it meant to be his daughter.

I remembered the rainy afternoon I'd gotten a call from his private physician, explaining my father had passed away. I went to find Gary and told my husband what had happened, lost between grief and disbelief.

That was the first time Gary hit me. And that was the first time I tried to leave him.

I'd been so stunned. I had no idea what happened or why. Then when Gary cried and apologized, I said okay.

I was not blinded by love. In fact, I didn't ever really love Gary. He was older, smarter, and I'd married him, so I thought I had to stay.

He'd convinced me that I needed him, and stupidly, I believed him. Gary flattered me when I needed attention, and I mistook it for love.

I figured if he loved me enough, maybe I would learn to love him too.

I mean, it wasn't like I had a slew of suitors. Shy, chubby women, even rich ones, didn't exactly have to fight them off with a bat.

After it became clear I was not inheriting the company, Gary's violent outbursts increased in frequency and potency.

Like most abusive assholes, he was not sorry.

The last time he hit me, he said he was going to teach me a lesson by hurting Sammy.

That was when I knew I hated him, and I needed to leave him.

I wouldn't let him hurt my son. And when he moved towards my baby's door, belt in hand, I did the only thing I could.

I covered my son's door with my body and refused to budge. He broke my arm, trying to pull me away. When I proved immovable, he used his belt.

That was my first black eye. And just where my hairline met my left cheek, I now carried a scar from where his buckle scored my skin.

Yeah, I could admit that I was dumb for sticking around as long as I did.

But for Sammy's sake, I got wise.

Over the last six months, with Meredith's help and the other women, along with some therapy, I found myself again. My true self. And I was healing.

I was starting to forgive myself. To trust myself.

But this last ditch effort by my ex to hurt me was unbearable.

I would never allow Gary access to our son.

No, I didn't have the power to make him go away, but I thought maybe I knew someone who did.

My stomach twisted in knots.

I hadn't told anyone about that evening after Andres had escorted me and Sammy home after our *Sourdough Sunday* lunch before Labor Day.

I kept the secret of how I basically threw myself at the sexiest man I had ever seen. Stunned when he reciprocated, catching me in his strong, burly arms, and kissing me so passionately, I almost combusted.

My ex didn't like aggressive women, and if ever I tried to initiate sex, he'd retaliate by humiliating me, making me feel bad for being human.

I was so tired of feeling bad about myself.

Andres had felt safe. He felt different. And when he watched me with hooded, stormy eyes, I wanted him.

So, I pounced. And he reacted.

We had sex in the tiny living room area of my makeshift apartment, and I'd been living with the guilt of that for two months now.

It was already late October. And ever since it happened, I haven't been able to stop thinking about him.

Andres was nothing like my ex. He wasn't soft and pasty. He was thick, muscled, and so damn hot.

I started things, but Andres took the reins almost immediately. He took *me* hard and deliberately.

Exactly like I needed him to.

Those heated, sea-foam-colored eyes of his never left me as he kissed, fondled, and fucked me until I could hardly remember my own name.

That night was incredible. For someone like me, whose only sexual experience came from a man who barely tolerated me, well, it was something I treasured.

I didn't know it could be like that.

But even so, I ignored his attempts to talk to me after. I just couldn't face him.

What must he think of me?

What kind of person had sex with a virtual stranger when she was living in a woman's shelter?

The therapist I'd been seeing, Dr. Ravnikar, told me I should never judge anyone, especially not myself, for my actions.

But it was hard not to.

I didn't have room for complications in my life, and Andres was definitely that.

Sammy needed me. And I needed my son to be safe.

Ironically, or maybe just because Fate was a cunt,

Andres was the only person I could think of who might be able to help.

Gary's threats were hanging over my head, and I didn't have anywhere else to turn.

Thunder rumbled outside, and I glanced out the small window.

Sammy was asleep, but he didn't like storms. I bit my lip as I grabbed my cell phone.

I didn't know if Andres would listen, but I hoped, and as I dialed, I prayed.

Please, just listen.

Two months passed since I'd been inside Ellie Maxwell's hot as fuck body.

Two months of unreturned calls and texts.

Two months of wet dreams that left me feeling unrested and horny as fuck.

Two long ass motherfucking months.

Goddamn.

I was losing my mind.

I'd only just been promoted to a position in Volkov Industries that not only meant the head honchos trusted me, but that they depended on me. They relied on me to make their business better.

Holy. Fucking. Shit.

I was just a guy from Hoboken who grew up with

his mom and stepfather in a one bedroom apartment where I slept on the fucking couch until I went off to college.

My parents did the best they could. After my stepdad died, my mom had to work, scrubbing floors while I busted my ass at school, and waited tables to pay for it all.

After I made my first million dollars, I bought the building my mother lived in. With the next million, I renovated it exactly how she wanted. By the next million, I hired Sigma International to see to the security system.

For a long time, my mother was the most important woman in my life. And I thought she would be forever. Until now.

It was different, of course. I wasn't Oedipus fucking Rex. Yes, I loved my mother. And I tried to be a good son to her.

But I was pretty goddamn certain I was one hundred percent head over fucking heels in love with Ellie Maxwell.

Ellie.

Sweet Ellie.

Why won't you let me in?

I knew she'd been through some shit. I hacked

into her private files over at St. E's the first time I met her.

It wasn't an easy job, but lucky for me, I got in before Meredith, that was Josef's wife, Josef Aziz, who happened to own Sigma International Security and was now a controlling partner at Volkov Industries, had Sigma take over the whole system at St. E's.

Getting in now would take more skill than I had, and I was pretty damn good. But goddamn, the shit I read about her. It made me seethe just thinking about it.

Yeah, I wanted to kill that piece of shit slimeball who put his hands on my woman.

I knew I shouldn't think about her like that—*as mine.*

She hadn't agreed. And I hadn't really asked. But I knew what it felt like to have my dick buried inside her tight wet heat, and to me, that made her mine.

Jesus. Christ.

The moment I thought of her sweet cunt squeezing my cock, I went rock hard. I hissed a sigh, closed my eyes, and reached between my legs to push my ever-growing boner down.

Two fucking months of the worst blue balls I've ever had, and that was saying something.

I was a skinny kid with acne and no money. I didn't get a lot of tail when I was a teenager. After high school though, well, that was another story.

Once I filled out, started hitting the gym between college classes and work, I had more women than I could keep track of.

My mom always told me my eyes were the clincher. I had blue-gray eyes and dark hair, and she thought it was a killer combo.

But I was pretty sure it had more to do with my thick dick and my appetite for pussy.

Not that I'd even looked at another woman since I saw her.

My Lupina.

Ellie Maxwell was a fucking goddess.

She had a body I could get lost in. Hell, I fucking dreamed about it night after night.

Thighs I could wrap even my large hands around, breasts perfect for sucking, and an ass that would not quit.

Fuck.

One taste. That was all I'd had, but I was a goddamn addict now. Even putting in stupid long hours couldn't stop my mind from drifting off at any given point.

The thing about it was I wanted her to come to me. To acknowledge this mutual attraction.

I wanted *her* to want *me*.

And yeah, I heard the Cheap Trick song in my head every fucking time I thought about it.

I mean, it went against the whole alpha male nature thing, right?

Like I knew everything in me was telling me to hunt her down and not give her a choice.

To make her my woman any way I could.

But that was too fucking close to how her *soon-to-be-dead-if-I get-my-way* ex treated her.

And I wouldn't do that to Ellie.

Not now. Not ever.

But I couldn't walk away either.

There was just something about her. Something untamed and wild behind her eyes. Something I recognized.

They said like attracts like, and I understood tenacity.

How else did the bastard son of a low level Bratva soldier reinvent himself the way I had?

I mean, come on. Even I had to admit, I had grit.

Yeah, I took my Hispanic stepfather's name.

Hell yeah.

The man raised me, and I was proud to be a

Ramirez. As for my sperm donor, well, that had been weighing heavily on my mind as of late.

I had yet to tell the Volkov brothers about our familial relationship. They didn't know my birth father was their uncle, their father's youngest brother whom I wasn't sure they'd ever even met.

He'd come to America with the crew he was involved with. Knocked up my mother and left her before he got himself killed.

I suppose that was for the best. My mother knew his name, and that was pretty much all she knew about him.

I had to tell Adrik and Marat. They deserved to know the reason I worked so hard to try to get them to notice me, turning down jobs I'd been offered at well established companies for the chance to work for them.

Yeah, I needed to come clean.

I knew it.

But I was distracted, what with Ellie coming into the picture and the way my brain was fucked over this whole thing with her. I just hadn't had the time.

The woman called to me like a siren's song. She was all I heard. All I saw. All I thought about.

She attracted me like no one else ever had. And

not because she ran away like a mystery in the night the way Sofia did with Adrik.

Not that at all.

I knew where she was. I knew exactly where that fine as fuck woman parked her sweet ass every night.

But what kind of fucking animal would I be if I stalked a woman on the run from her abusive ex?

That motherfucker should be dead already.

I growled and tried to focus back on work. I couldn't just kill the man.

Not yet anyway.

I opened my cell phone to check the security feed outside the Morristown home she was living in.

Yeah, I fucking hacked it. But I was smarter about it. I merely swiped one of Josef's men's passwords.

I had no choice, really.

I couldn't rest until I knew she was safe and sound inside. I scanned the feed until I found her returning from the park with Sammy.

That kid was a real cutie. I was crazy about him already. Almost four years old and smart as a whip.

But his mother. Holy hell, she looked beautiful. Her pixie cut had grown out, and the dark curls framing her face were half wild from the fall breeze.

Those hazel eyes were sparkling with joy as she

held her son's hand and walked inside, greeting Mrs. Stevens as she did.

The woman was hired by Sigma International and had all the training necessary for doing a job like that. Her military background ensured she was tough enough to deal with any unwanted visitors that might try to bully their way in.

Still, I'd much rather she was here with me. I'd bought a house close enough to where she was staying that I could be there at a moment's notice.

Was that weird?

I didn't really fucking care.

I just knew I wasn't parking my ass all the way in Manhattan while Ellie and Sammy were all the way out here in fucking New Jersey. Her cunt of an ex was still walking around free, and I just couldn't bring myself to get any farther than this.

Three houses.

That was it.

I was three fucking houses down, and I made sure she didn't fucking see me coming and going. It was a good thing I kept the crazy hours that I did.

My phone rang. The sound was loud in the nearly empty space I'd claimed as an office.

Morristown was filled with big, old houses, and

this one wasn't exactly for sale when I approached the owner. But everyone had a price.

All I needed was a desk, a chair, and a bed. My real stuff was back in my condo in New York.

Ring. Ring. Ring.

I looked down. My heart was hammering inside my chest, and I wasn't sure why, but it felt like something was about to happen.

Something that could maybe change my life.

I heaved a sigh, slightly annoyed at the interruption.

Not that I was doing anything.

Well, anything other than obsessing over Ellie.

Glancing down, I exited the security feed I'd had paused on my cell phone.

Ignoring the sudden urge to get a screenshot of the zoomed in image of her elfin face, I swiped up to close the app and checked the ID of the caller.

Unknown?

My heart stuttered beneath my breastbone as I pressed the green button.

"Hello?"

I knew Ellie had been given an untraceable burner phone upon entry to the shelter, and she was the only person with an *Unknown Caller* ID who had my phone number.

I'd made sure of that.

"Andres? It's me."

Her voice sounded tinny through the cheap phone, but I closed my eyes on the wave of emotion that filled me at hearing her say my name.

Ellie called me.

She called *me.*

"Yeah, it's me. Is everything okay?" I asked, clearing my throat a little.

"Yes. Well, not really," she replied.

"Which is it? Yes or no? Ellie, do you need me to send a security team?"

I already had my backup phone in my hand, ready to send an alert to Sigma, and slipping my shoes back on my feet.

"No, no. Um, I was wondering, would you, that is, if you don't have anything better to do—"

Her voice sounded muffled, like she was covering her mouth. Maybe from embarrassment? I canted my head, trying to decipher what the heck was going on.

"Ellie. Spit it out."

"Would you be willing to marry me?" she blurted, and fuck me, I almost fell out of my chair.

Well. Shit.

Whatever I thought she was going to ask, that wasn't it.

"Oh my God! I'm being dumb. I'm sorry. Um, forget I said—"

No way. She wasn't getting out of this that easily.

"I'm coming over," I said, ending the call.

It was like all the noise just got sucked out of the room. And the only thing I could hear was the sound of my own breathing and my heart beating.

That wild attraction, the insane force I felt towards Ellie, was pulling me.

All I knew was that it was important I moved. That I took that first step.

Closer to the door.

Closer to the street.

Closer to the rest of my life.

Closer to her.

Oh my fuck.

"I think I just lost my mind," I mumbled, dropping my cell phone on the plain coffee table that sat in the middle of the living room like it was hot.

I just asked Andres Ramirez to marry me.

What the shit?

I can't believe I did that.

What the hell was I thinking?

Okay, so I kind of knew what I was thinking. The crumpled up letter and envelope sitting on the tiny table where Sammy and I ate most of our meals glared at me in the dimly lit room.

Andres was a man.

Duh.

He was big, tall, strong, wealthy, and powerful.

I wasn't mercenary. It was just, well, I grew up with money, so I recognized it.

He didn't strike me as the kind of man who always had it. But his expensive clothes, the fact he worked for Volkov Industries and was crowned their *prince of acquisitions* told me everything I needed to know.

So, me asking him to marry me was more about having him in my arsenal as a weapon to use against my ex-husband than the fact I couldn't stop thinking about him.

And his big, fat cock.

Seriously, the man was hung, and he knew how to use it.

Oh my God. What was wrong with me?

I squealed and covered my eyes.

Okay, reality check. Gary was a motherfucking slimeball.

He wasn't above hitting women and threatening children. And he sure as fuck wasn't above suing me, like he was doing now. And not just for custody. For money.

The man who beat me wanted me to pay him.

So, I wasn't wrong when I said I needed help.

I needed someone on my side. A weapon of my own. I needed Andres Ramirez.

That Andres and I had already had sex once was just a bonus. I knew we were compatible.

I knew I could at least give him something for what I was asking and no, I had no delusions that I was anything special.

I wasn't conceited.

I was just a single mom who needed to protect her son.

That Andres seemed to be a little bit into me, *like nine inches into me,* was a bonus.

Fuck.

He was on his way over, and I really needed to stop thinking about his dick.

If I was being honest, I'd just admit I thought Andres was hot as hell and I wouldn't mind spreading my legs for him again.

He was so damn sexy.

The man turned me on without even trying to. It was just something about him, all that muted strength and power. Almost like violence flowed in his veins, brewing in his stormy blue-gray eyes.

I'd never seen eyes like that on a man. At times, they looked positively opaque. Like cat eyes.

Cats. Fuck.

Rescuing Rocky was likely the biggest mistake I'd made in recent months. Well, after fucking Andres. Or maybe after proposing to him.

Shit.

I sneezed, clenching my thighs so I didn't accidentally pee myself. That was a gift from Mother Nature after I gave birth to my son. That and my love handles.

Yeah, giving birth wrecked my pelvic floor, and I had no idea what a fucking Kegel was. The internet said I needed to imagine picking up a marble with my pelvic muscles, and ever since I read that I stopped trying.

Why the fuck would I put a small ass marble up my vagina? No, thank you.

I was like ninety-nine percent sure Kegel exercises were made up. Probably by someone without a pelvic floor.

Oh my shit, I am spiraling.

Rocky ran across the room at that moment, kicking up dander and dust.

So, of fucking course I sneezed again.

"Dammit," I growled and ran to the bathroom to change my stupid clothes.

I hadn't intended to put on my pjs until after Andres left, but oh well.

Fuck it.

Halloween attire from Walmart was going to have to do for the fancy as fuck man.

Yeah, I was definitely allergic.

I felt itchy every time I touched the little beast, but in all honesty, he was a cute little guy.

His fur was a deep, chocolate brown, and he had three white paws and a white line down his face.

Like rocky road ice cream with marshmallows on top. Sammy's favorite flavor. Hence the name.

The kitten made Sammy happy, so I was keeping him.

Even if I had to wear pads because I was constantly sneeze-peeing.

And if Andres said yes to my proposal, then he would have to keep him, too.

The intercom buzzed just as I yanked my tank top over my head. Fluffing my hair quickly, I slid across the floor in my sock-covered feet and pressed the button.

"Ellie? There's someone downstairs for you, dear. A Mr. Ramirez?"

Mrs. Stevens' voice sounded fuzzy through the intercom speaker. Each floor had one right by the newly installed, double locked doors Meredith had the construction crew put in.

She'd managed to create five units out of one house, and the result was literally perfect for the people who would be staying there. So far, it was just me and Sammy and Mrs. Stevens.

"Ellie?"

Shit. I forgot to answer. Unsure of what to say. I settled on keeping it simple.

"Um, thank you. Mrs. Stevens. Can he come up, please?"

"He is on Mrs. Aziz's approved visitor list, so yes, he can, but I wanted to check with you first."

"Thank you, Mrs. Stevens. I appreciate it."

"No problem, dear. Don't forget we have a strict eleven PM curfew on visitors."

"Yes, Mrs. Stevens. I won't forget," I said honestly.

I wouldn't forget.

I had half an hour to talk to Andres about my preposterous idea. A full thirty minutes with which to make a total ass of myself.

Shit.

How was I supposed to forget that?

Speaking of time, how the heck did he get here so fast?

I ran my hand over my messy hair. It was still damp from my shower, and longer than I've had it in years.

I had on zero makeup, and a tank top over baggy flannel pants with little pumpkins all over them. I never did get any of my wardrobe back after leaving Gary's condo.

Of course, he lied when the lawyers asked about

it. He said I took everything of Sammy's and mine with me.

As if I could have done that with a broken arm. No, the sonofabitch destroyed it all.

It didn't matter.

Stuff was just stuff, and I was happier in my Walmart PJs than I was in the long silk gowns he insisted I wear to bed.

Nightgowns sucked. Long ones did, anyway.

I was not a restful sleeper and all that tossing and turning meant I'd get tangled up in the skirts of those gowns.

Another thing I did that annoyed Gary, by the way, which was another reason he started using a separate bedroom.

I never saw the evil in him until the end. He was good at making it seem like everything was my fault.

I was the reason he couldn't sleep in the same bed as me.

I was the reason he wasn't interested in sex with me after I conceived our son.

After, well, the baby weight disgusted him. Not that I'd ever been skinny.

I was also the reason he worked so much. Quite closely, in fact, with his thin blonde secretary.

Everything was my fault.

And it wasn't until he hit me that I put it together. All the little things, the slights, and the insults he'd tossed at me over the three and a half years we were together, were all a distraction.

Things he said and did to cover up the fact he was a total slimeball.

I didn't deserve any of it. The way he treated me was a reflection of his poor character, not mine.

I understood that now. And I wasn't going to let him get away with it anymore.

With my inheritance tied up, I couldn't afford the lawyers I knew I needed to fight him. These new threats involving my son?

I couldn't even think about them.

The idea of my ex getting his slimy hands on my precious child—*no.*

Just no.

Maybe I should've been paying more attention to why I thought of Andres the second I read the letter of intent to sue for visitation from Gary's lawyer. But it was too late to worry about that now.

I listened as heavy footsteps stopped on the landing outside my door.

Andres was here.

Too late to chicken out now.

St. Elizabeth's offsite housing was actually an old Victorian remodeled to offer five smallish apartments, if you counted the basement apartment where Mrs. Stevens, the caretaker, stayed.

Each one was big enough for two people to share. In Ellie's case that meant her and Sammy.

There was nothing wrong with the house. It was fine. But my hackles went up every time I thought about her living there.

It was boorish of me, I knew that. But I couldn't help it. Ellie deserved better. She deserved the best. She deserved me.

It wasn't conceit that had me calling myself the

best. It was fact. No one else could possibly feel about that woman the way I did.

She was all I thought about. Everything I saw, heard, smelled, felt.

It was all her.

All Ellie.

And. She. Was. Everything. To. Me.

Yeah, I was sick. Borderline fucking psycho. But what could I say?

Ellie and me, we were simply meant to be. I believed that with every fiber of my being.

I lifted my fist and knocked quietly. Half a second later, she pulled the door open, and my mouth went dry.

She was wearing a pair of Halloween-themed flannel pants and a simple cotton tank top. Nothing fancy or sexy.

But the swell of her breasts and the hard nubs of her nipples pressing against her top still made my mouth fucking water.

She's perfect.

Her hair was tousled, and her face looked like she'd just scrubbed it clean.

She smelled good. Fresh and clean like soap and body lotion.

There was nothing obviously seductive about

what she had on or how she looked.

But I was captivated.

Completely and totally.

That invisible magnetic pull I'd felt towards her since the first time I ever laid eyes on Ellie was in full force. I couldn't look away if I tried.

My cock began to stir, and it was only through sheer will alone I managed to stand there and not reach for her.

"Come in," she said, her voice low and scratchy like she was nervous, and her mouth had gone dry.

Concern had me furrowing my brows, but I bit my tongue, waiting for her to get the ball rolling.

"Can I get you something to drink or a snack?" she asked, and I shook my head.

I followed her deeper inside the room, ignoring the wall and the couch where we'd gone at each other like a couple of hormone-crazed teenagers.

"I guess I should start by explaining why I called you," she began.

"I thought that was to propose?" I said, my lips quirked up in a half smile I hoped was charming and not psychotic.

I exhaled a sigh of relief when she responded with a mock-dirty look and rolled her pretty hazel eyes, gesturing for me to take a seat at the small card table where I imagined she and Sammy shared meals.

"Yeah, about that. First, I should explain," she began, but was interrupted by a lightning fast ball of chocolate colored fur.

Ellie jumped, covering her nose, when the small cat jumped into my lap.

"Who's this?" I asked, charmed by the animal.

"That's Rocky, Sammy's new kitten," she said, still covering her nose.

She sat with her legs tightly crossed, and I frowned, petting the kitten and placing him gently on the floor.

"He's cute. But, um, are you okay?"

"Me?" she said, her voice muffled by her hands. She dropped them, wiping her mouth and tucking her hair behind her ears.

So fucking cute.

"Yeah, um, allergies."

She said, and I frowned, making a mental note to research cat allergies.

"So, anyway, I don't know how much you know about my past," she started again.

I sat across from Ellie, my attention on her as she explained what I already knew from my clandestine research.

She was newly divorced after fleeing her abusive ex with her only son.

I listened quietly, allowing her to finish, and pretending that I hadn't already read every bit of information I could find on Ellie Maxwell and Gary Peters.

It wasn't like I could interrupt her. Besides, it was probably cathartic.

Ellie was a survivor. A goddamn warrior. And I was so fucking proud of her.

But I wouldn't tell her I knew all about it.

I mean, how would I even begin to explain the lines I'd crossed?

I couldn't.

So I didn't even try.

"My father was an important businessman. But he was old-fashioned, and he was a lot older by the time I was born. His ideas of what was appropriate for a female were seriously outdated, but I didn't know any better, and really, my interests were always a bit different," she said, and I leaned closer.

Maybe she was right.

I never heard her talk about what she liked and disliked before. Those were secret things. Things I longed for her to share with me because she wanted to.

"I didn't really push to finish college. I had my own reading preferences, and I enjoyed cooking, baking, and crafts. I know I seem simple and maybe even dumb, but it was what I liked—"

"Hey, don't call yourself that. But liked? As in past tense?" I couldn't help but interrupt.

"Oh, well, I don't know. I mean, I still like cooking. But, well, it's been a long time since I thought about what I liked," she mumbled, frowning.

I wanted to reach across the distance between us and smooth out the lines on her forehead.

Ellie should never frown. She should only smile.

I could learn what makes her smile.

"Um, the point I was making is maybe some of the fault for my failed marriage is on me—"

"No," I said, suddenly furious. "Don't you dare blame yourself for anything that happened between you and that pitiful fucking excuse for a human being."

"I-I just meant that maybe Gary was expecting someone with more sophisticated tastes and business understanding. Not to mention a better inheritance. But my father never intended for me to run the company. Gary assumed marrying me would make him a shoo-in. But it didn't, and he hated me for it," she stated.

"Ellie, I think I should probably interrupt you here and explain that I know all about your father's will and the state of the company. Josef already asked me to dig into Maxwell Mining."

"He did?"

"Yes. I hope that is okay with you. It's sort of what I do for Volkov Industries. Acquire businesses in trouble. Root out the problems. Make them better. Make them earn. Sorry, um, please continue," I said.

"Right," she began, "so, I don't know if his intentions towards me were anything other than mercenary, and I feel stupid for not knowing. Leaving him was necessary. He, uh, he," she paused.

"Ellie, it's okay," I whispered her name.

I was caught between wanting her to continue and not wanting it. I couldn't just sit there and listen to her tell me how this man hurt her.

Not without wanting to kill him.

But Ellie needed me to listen. She needed someone to lean on, and I could do that. For her, I would do that.

So, I forced myself to be still and silent while she had her say.

I watched her, helpless to do anything else, while she wrung her hands together and shrugged. She lifted her tear filled golden green eyes to mine, and my heart damn near broke.

Rage turned my vision red, but it wasn't directed at her.

Never that.

I was going to destroy her ex. His fate was sealed the moment he touched her. Gary Peters was living on borrowed time. He just didn't know it yet.

And that was what made it fun.

I'd already used my computer skills to check up on the bastard. He'd been double dealing at work, cheating in his business, and on his now ex-wife, and squirreling away Ellie's money for years.

She didn't act like it, but the woman was worth half a billion dollars easily. And after I finished fucking up his plans to mess with Maxwell Mining and her inheritance, my sweet Lupina would be worth double that.

I was already going to fix that for her, whether or not she was interested in me. That she proposed tonight just solidified my tentative plans.

It was the push I needed to go forward. The gunshot at the start of what was going to be a very long and intense race.

"Gary is seeking visitation rights with Sammy," she whispered, as if saying the thing aloud might make it true. "H-his lawyers informed me that's just the first step. He is planning to sue for full custody claiming I am an unfit mother. With my inheritance tied up, I can't fight him. I don't have the means—"

"Do you need money, Ellie?" I said, hating myself for making the offer.

"I won't lie. Yes, I need money. But, you see, part of his claim is that I *am* a liar. A liar, unreliable, flippant, he used all sorts of words to describe me, claiming I was never there for Sammy. But it's not true," she said, her eyes blazing with anger.

Good. I could take her anger. It was her sadness and fear that were knives in my gut.

"I know you're a good mother, Ellie. Anyone who knows you can see that."

"That's the thing. I didn't notice at first, but over the last few years Gary managed to separate me from anyone who might have been on my side. I never had close girlfriends, but even so, I haven't seen or talked to anyone who knew me before I married him in years," she explained.

Fuck.

That bastard had isolated Ellie. Making her dependent on him, not just for money, but for companionship.

Goddamn it.

He'd done what classic narcissists and abusers did. He made her feel beholden to him for even the tiniest crumb of attention.

He was going to fucking pay for that.

It made me glad I'd already started bleeding his offshore accounts. Slowly, of course, so no one would notice.

I wondered how Gary would feel to know his stolen cash was going to help homeless women and children across the globe. Maybe I would tell him before I killed him.

Rat fucking bastard.

Ellie sniffed, and I refocused on her. The kitten was back, rubbing against my ankles, but I left him alone. I needed her to keep talking to me.

"His lawyer is claiming I'm histrionic, that I made everything up. He said Gary never hit me or threatened my son. That I threw myself down some stairs and gave myself a broken arm and bruises. I never filed a police report," she confessed.

I already knew that. So I said nothing. But Ellie misread my silence as judgment.

"Look, at the time I didn't care about Gary getting into trouble. I just cared about getting Sammy to safety," she defended herself.

"You did what you had to, Ellie. I'm so damn

proud of you. Now explain how I can help," I said, not giving her a chance to respond to my praise.

"Gary's lawyer is saying I can't offer Sammy a stable home. Apparently, Gary is engaged to his former secretary, and he can. He has money. He still has a job with Maxwell Mining until the company is sold. He has a home, and in a week, he will have a new wife, and a prospective mother for my son."

"I understand," I said, and I did.

"Andres, I'm sorry. What I am asking you for isn't fair—"

I couldn't let her finish that sentence, so instead, I reached out across the table and grabbed her hand.

"When do you want to get married?"

"What?"

"We can fly to Vegas. Or we can have a small ceremony right here with just a few people. I have friends at city hall. We can have all the paperwork and the wedding license signed in time for the weekend."

"You would do that?" she asked.

I nodded.

Fuck. Yes.

I would do that for her. That and so much more.

It was probably a good thing Ellie had no idea what I was willing to do to secure her as mine.

"Before you agree, I have to ask you something," I said, and she nodded. "Is this the way you want to do it, or do you just want me to make him stop?"

"W-what do you mean?"

Her voice wasn't more than a whisper, and I could practically hear her heart pounding.

I shouldn't have asked that. Shouldn't have given her a way out. But it was too late now.

So, I continued.

"You know what I mean, Ellie. Do you want me to make your ex stop?"

Thunder pounded in my brain as I waited for her to respond.

The woman of my dreams had just asked me to marry her, and like an asshole I offered her another option.

I guess what they said was true, love was blind, deaf, and dumb.

So fucking dumb.

Ellie blinked slowly before sliding her hand across the table. She touched mine, holding it, then gripping it, and I closed my eyes for a moment just to steady myself.

Fuck.

I never realized how good it would feel to have her reach for me. I wished it was for something other than this, but I would take it.

I would take it and hold on to it with both fucking hands.

"I don't want Gary to ever have the power to threaten or hurt my son. But he's Sammy's father. Plus, he's a well-known businessman. People would notice if something happened. And, Andres, I don't want you to get in trouble."

"Okay. Then let's do it. Let's get married. And you will let me deal with this for you, won't you Ellie?"

"You would really do that?" she asked, wide-eyed and so fucking beautiful she stole my breath.

I nodded, and she inhaled, looking down at her hands.

"Yes, I would do that. I promise I won't let him hurt either of you ever again. Do you trust me?" I asked, my heart practically hammering me to death.

Christ. She's so precious.

Her answer was so goddamn important to me.

I waited impatiently, my eyes fixed on her downcast face. Then, suddenly, she lifted her gaze to mine and her shoulders relaxed.

"Yes, Andres. I trust you."

I had no idea a couple of words could mean so much to me. I closed my eyes and exhaled the breath I'd been holding.

Then I took hold of her hand once more and lifted it to my lips, kissing her knuckles.

"Then, to answer your initial question, *yes*, Ellie Maxwell, I'll marry you."

"Wow! You look so beautiful!"

I'd been looking at my reflection in a giant full-sized mirror, trying to see if I recognized the creature staring back at me, when I caught Meredith staring at me with a huge grin on her face.

I didn't, by the way. Recognize myself, that was. I mean, this was a version of me I'd always wanted to be.

Someone pretty and confident. Someone who belonged. Who had family and support. Who had found their person.

It's all pretend. Don't forget that, Ellie.

Sometimes, I really hated my inner voice. Logic was such a goddamn bitch.

I knew this wasn't the fairytale wedding it was dressed up to be. But still. Couldn't my inner voice just shut up long enough for me to enjoy today?

"Ellie, come on. Smile. You really look amazing," Meredith repeated the sentiment and crossed the room.

"Really? Cause I feel like a crazy person," I hissed, two seconds from a panic attack.

When Andres asked if I wanted to fly to Vegas or get married here, I chose here so we didn't disrupt Sammy too much.

But I had no idea he meant *get married,* as in like have a huge ass wedding with all the frills.

It seemed the second he said yes, and I agreed to stay to do it here, Andres had started the ball rolling.

Apparently, my soon-to-be hubby was a sucker for a party. He was also protective as fuck, something I was eternally grateful for.

Sammy and I were hustled from St. E's in Morristown to Andres' condo on Billionaire's Row in Central Park. Our new luxurious digs were in the same building where Meredith and her husband, as well as the Volkov brothers, owned their own condos.

It was incredible, and that the building was more secure than Fort Knox was just a bonus. I didn't have to worry about Gary or any of his hired goons making appearances.

Really, I shouldn't complain. The condo was amazing. Apart from all the protection, there was just so much room.

The view alone was breathtaking. All of Manhattan was spread out below us in full color like a miniature model set. The furniture was masculine, yes, but it was also of excellent quality.

Everything was neat and clean, and at first, I worried about bringing Rocky, but Andres had insisted it was okay.

In fact, on the day we moved Andres had already installed an entire wall full of cat climbers and scratchers for the little furball in the living room. He promised Sammy more to come, but he wanted him to help pick everything out.

Sammy was thrilled. But I worried about the dangers of cat dander. Silly me to think Andres hadn't thought of that.

He had a bottle of allergy meds waiting for me. They were recommended by New York's top ENT center, where he'd made me an appointment. He also assured me with Rocky on a new, special diet and with regular grooming, my reaction to the cat's fur and dander should get much better.

It was thoughtful.

It was something no one had ever really done for me.

And I didn't know what to do with that.

Andres gave the two of us space to settle in. He even hired an interior designer who sat with the two of us and Sammy so we could choose things for his bedroom, turning the otherwise simple guest room into a little boy's paradise.

"You don't have to do all this," I said.

"Of course, I do."

"You are doing more than enough just giving us a place to stay."

"I am not giving you a place to stay, Lupina. We will discuss that later. But being able to provide for you and Sammy is my pleasure. Don't fight me on this."

We never did *discuss that later,* but every day since, I'd thought about those words. I thought about everything he'd done and was going to do. Like marry me.

Still, I never expected a real wedding.

Complete with gown, tuxes, flowers, bridesmaids, the works.

I mean, his mother was there, for Christ's sake.

It was too much.

It was amazing.

That Andres had quietly insisted on participating in the decorating touched something inside me.

I could almost allow myself to believe he was invested in this, in us.

But I put a lid on all that messy emotion really quick.

I just couldn't afford to be charmed by my almost husband.

I had yet to discover his motivation for going along with all this craziness. But I wouldn't fall for thinking it was because of me.

I'd made that mistake before. Whatever Andres wanted, I would gladly give him if I could. If it was my inheritance, fine. I would do anything to secure Sammy's well-being.

Maybe he was doing this because he thought he would benefit since I was friends with the *wives of wolves*. The women married to his bosses.

That was what my brand new friend group jokingly referred to themselves as.

"Well? What's that look for?" Meredith asked.

I closed my eyes, then met her questioning stare. Truth was, I didn't know what I was doing, and I had to confide in someone.

"Am I doing the right thing?"

I bit my lip, chewing off the lipstick I'd just carefully applied. I stared at Meredith instead of my reflection because it was easier that way.

If I saw my wedding dress, it would just make me spiral all over again.

I didn't know how he knew, but Andres had managed to get me the perfect dress. He'd sent a half dozen gowns in varying lengths and styles to the guest bedroom where I was sleeping until the wedding.

He'd said it was a sort of wedding gift. I never knew a husband to choose his wife's gown, but Andres had impeccable taste. That he seemed to have an instinct for what I liked was just luck.

They'd all been beautiful.

All my size.

And none of them were white.

In fact, hardly any of them were what people considered appropriate for a wedding. But we were getting hitched on Halloween and it looked like Andres was a themed wedding kind of guy.

So, yeah, I wore black on my wedding day.

Head to toe black.

And for the first time in maybe ever, I felt gorgeous.

It was not my norm. Not what was expected of me or what I'd been taught to be by others.

"You mean are you doing the right thing by marrying super-hot Andres so he can protect you and your son from your sleazy ex, and maybe give you some sweaty time between the sheets while he's doing that? Is that the right thing you are referring to?" Meredith asked.

"Oh my God. Why did I even tell you about that?" I grumbled, annoyed with myself.

I'd kept it a secret for so long, but when I announced I was marrying Andres, I had to give the girls something. So, I told them about the amazing sex we'd had a few months ago.

"Look, Ellie, it's perfectly natural for two people who find each other attractive to want to have sex. So if you feel the mood strike, you just walk up to him, grab him by his dick and say *get on the bed, bitch, mama wants to go for a ride,*" she finished, waggling her eyebrows.

"Meredith! Please stop talking," I yelled her name, then mumbled the rest, closing my eyes.

"Ellie," she mocked me. "Seriously, you are marrying *Andres*. He is like the sweetest man ever. Have you seen him playing with Sammy? I mean, how could you go wrong?" she asked.

Immediately, my mind filled with images of Andres and my son.

Andres bringing home toys and books for Sammy to play with.

Andres kneeling on the floor in his gorgeous custom suit to give Sammy a high-five.

Andres laughing when Sammy got his finger-paint covered hands on his briefcase.

Andres tucking him in at night.

"Okay. You're right. It will be fine," I whispered.

I wanted to believe it.

I needed to believe it.

But what if he turned out to be a prick? What if he just wanted to control me like Gary?

All my life I did what I was told. I was demure, submissive, quiet.

Prim.

Proper.

Liar.

Yeah, I was a liar. And I was so fucking sick of it.

So tired of trying to meet others' expectations and falling short.

So weary of pretending.

But Andres didn't ask me to pretend.

In fact, if I were being honest with myself, Andres didn't ask me for a thing. If he had any expectations of me, well, he hadn't said anything.

Except for that one little thing.

I squirmed. My heart tightened.

"Look, I don't know how it all happened so fast, but I've seen the way he looks at you, Ellie. That man is into you," Meredith continued.

"What? Oh, no. I already told you, he's just helping me out. We don't have feelings for each other," I scoffed.

"Uh huh. Tell yourself that if it helps, but if Andres is anything like the others, there is more to it than that," Meredith chided gently.

"Have you seen Sammy?" I asked, changing the subject.

"He's with Michaela and Lucy in the playroom. Nanny Rosa is with them," Meredith said, stifling a yawn.

It was early days in her pregnancy, but I frowned and pointed to a chair.

"Put your butt in that seat, please. I don't need you passing out before I make it down the aisle."

It was my turn to scold, but Meredith simply grinned. She patted her still flat tummy and sat down on the chaise lounge.

The ceremony was taking place in Meredith's enormous backyard. She and Josef bought a house out on Long Island close to the others a few weeks ago.

It was gorgeous, and the weather was perfect for an outdoor ceremony.

Four days had passed since he'd whisked me and Sammy away to his condo, and I'd barely seen him except to sign papers, or when he joined us for meals, and to tuck Sammy in at night.

Eating together should have felt strange at first, but he made it seem so normal.

When I made a simple spaghetti dinner the first night at his place, I wasn't expecting Andres to join us.

But he had.

He sat right down and dug in, complimenting my homemade sauce, and asking for seconds. Sammy was delighted with his company. Not shy at all.

I'd been too stunned to protest when he stacked the dishes in the dishwasher and insisted on putting away the leftovers himself.

My soon-to-be husband was one surprise after another.

I'd been on edge, waiting for the next shoe to drop. But Andres hadn't asked me to change my habits or behave in a certain way.

He'd simply sent me these gowns with a note saying he couldn't wait to see what I chose.

The labels read Van Wong, and I recognized the couture designer as being from New York.

It was sorta wild. Crazy even.

But it felt right, so I went with it. The gown I chose was an absolute dream. The sleeves were made out of tight, sheer lace and came down to a V on the top part of my hand.

The neckline was also a deep V, and there were clingy little cups sewed inside to lift my average-sized boobs, making the most of my cleavage.

It was so soft and flowy, the skirt fell from my cinched waist in a dozen sheer back layers, one on top of the other, swishing around my calves and making me feel like I was walking through fluffy silk clouds.

I looked good. And I felt sexy.

I was just nervous as fuck.

Who wouldn't be in my shoes?

"Guys? Ten minutes," Destiny sang out, barreling into the bedroom.

"EEEEEEEK! You look so good! Andres is going to shit himself!" she squealed with glee.

"Oh my God! I hope not," Meredith snickered.

"It's an expression," Des replied, rolling her eyes.

"Yeah, a gross one."

"Okay, that's enough. It is my wedding day and I say be kind to one another, ladies," I said, ever the diplomat.

Sofia walked in next, and her smile matched the others when she looked at me in my dress. I turned to face her, nervously touching the cream-colored Gerbera daisy pinned in my hair along with some greenery instead of a veil.

"Oh, Ellie, you look amazing."

She handed me the matching bouquet, and grinned. I faced the women. All three of them were dressed in beautiful, simple, tea length dresses.

They were ivory silk with matching belts made

of silver, blue, and pink, and black ribbons tied around their waists. Those ribbons were a theme in the decorations as well.

I just loved them.

Their bouquets matched mine. Cream colored Gerbera daisies and a wealth of greenery with the same silver, blue, pink, and black ribbons trailing from them.

Oh, and the best part, everything was sprayed with glitter. Tons of it. And I had to admit I loved that, too.

"Are you ready?" Sof asked, and I looked at each woman, one by one.

Sof, Des, and Mer were the real *wives of wolves.* These women were fiercely loved and protected by their men.

They knew the deal with me and Andres. They knew I'd asked him to marry me to help protect my son.

I didn't count as one of them. But looking at them, I felt this longing in my soul. This horrible hope that maybe, just maybe, I could be.

I swallowed.

"We, um, we got you a little something, Ellie," Meredith said, stepping away from the others, her hand outstretched.

I looked down at the tiny box and frowned, opening it.

"Oh wow," I said.

Inside was a gold locket on a thin chain. There was a moon and a howling wolf carved on it with intricately woven vines and flowers. When I opened it, I almost cried. Inside was a picture of Sammy, his face turned up in a bright smile, and on the other side, was me and Andres.

I don't know where they found that picture, but I recognized the shirt as the one I had on. It was the one I wore at that same *Sourdough Sunday* lunch when Andres took me home.

The day I, *well*, the day I jumped him.

I closed the locket and traced the wolf carved on the outside.

"Here, let me put it on you," Meredith said, and I turned around and allowed her to place the chain around my neck.

Was Andres a wolf?

Was he like the others? Like those big, possessive alpha men who were totally obsessed with their wives?

I'd only heard whispers about their husbands.

The things they were capable of. The things they'd done to protect their women, and I wondered.

Hell.

I had no idea if Andres was a wolf or not. But he wasn't obsessed with me.

Why would he be?

I shook my head. I was being silly. We weren't getting married for the usual reasons.

Andres was simply a good man. He was just doing me a kindness. Probably more for Sammy's sake than mine.

He stepped up to help when I asked, and he was offering protection to me and Sammy.

After the wedding, I would find out what he really wanted in return.

I mean, we talked about some things. Like the fact we were both open to a real marriage. As in, *sex* was something we both wanted.

Oh God. Sex with my almost husband.

My body had no problem remembering what it was like the one and only time we'd had sex. And yeah, if the moisture between my thighs was anything to go by, my body was more than willing to do it again.

And again.

Shit. Stop. Think of anything else.

I needed to concentrate on the positives of having him for a husband.

Andres was kind.

He was patient.

Brilliant.

Protective.

And there is also the little fact he fucked like a god.

Fuck. I shouldn't have even bothered with underwear.

"**W**ell, you clean up nice," Josef said, standing next to me as I waited at the makeshift altar for my bride.

I appreciated him offering the use of his magnificent backyard to host our nuptials. It was huge and private, and the planner had done a fantastic job.

I wanted to give Ellie everything she wanted, and she'd mentioned liking it here. Josef and Meredith were accommodating, and Sammy was even going to spend the night so we could have a sort of honeymoon.

True, I hadn't talked much with Ellie over the last few days. I was busy seeing to all the arrangements.

Also, I didn't want to give her the chance to back out.

Oh, I made sure I was there for dinner every night. I wanted to make sure Sammy got acclimated to his new home, and to offer support and praise when he picked out stuff for his new room.

That I loved that kid and thought of him as mine already was just icing.

I mean, how could I not love him? He came from Ellie.

He looked just like her. That boy was a total sweetheart.

Bright and brave. I looked forward to spending more time with him. To being a father to him, even though we hadn't really talked about my role in his life.

I had every intention of making this family, my family, real. Ellie might need some time before she believed me, but she would get there. I'd help her as unobtrusively as possible.

Sammy seemed to like me well enough. Which was awesome. Kids were the best judges of character. I knew what it was like to be protective of my mother, and Sammy already showed signs where Ellie was concerned.

He probably saw more than she thought, but he wouldn't have to deal with any of that anymore.

I was here now, and I would protect him. Give

him a life any kid would be lucky to have, filled with warmth, security, and happiness.

I just had to figure out how to kill his sperm donor and not freak Ellie out.

Step one was getting her to date me. But that was moot since she asked me to marry her.

Being a father to Sammy was one of the perks of being with Ellie. And being with her was everything.

I checked my watch and sucked in a breath. We were starting any minute now.

Just seconds away from putting my last name on her, from sliding my ring onto her finger, where it would stay, and I swear to fuck, I was shaking with nerves.

Goddamn.

Anxiety skittered up my spine, and I flexed my hands, trying hard not to show it. This was the most important moment of my life.

The moment I become a husband and a father.

"Relax, the wedding is the easy part," Adrik said, joining us with Marat on his heels.

"Take it easy. You're like family, bro. We got you," Marat added.

"Um, I know this is short notice, but since I'm about to become a married man, I figured it's as good a time as any to confess something—"

"Confess? What are you talking about?" Adrik asked.

"Well, um, you mentioned I was like family. So, you know how my last name is Ramirez?"

"Yeah."

"Actually, that was my stepfather's name."

"Oh, yeah?" Marat said, sipping from his tumbler of whiskey.

"Yeah. My biological father's surname was Volkov."

Marat made a choking sound, turned his head, spitting out the ice cube he almost choked on.

Adrik just glared at me with his dark, unwavering stare.

As for Josef, well, he just whistled.

"Our father did not cheat—"

"Not your father. Your uncle. Ivan Volkov. He was my biological father. I never met him, but his name was on my birth certificate and my mother told me all about it when I turned sixteen and found it in a desk drawer."

"So, you are saying what, Andres? All this time, you worked for me, and I didn't know you are our cousin," Adrik said, his voice deep and low.

I tipped my chin and exhaled a breath.

"That's what I am saying," I said, looking at Adrik for a reaction.

"Excuse me, gentlemen, the ladies are ready to start," the officiant, an older man who worked at my mother's church, interrupted us with a genuine smile on his face.

I nodded my head in his direction to show I'd heard him and waited for him to walk away before directing my attention back to the men standing in front of me.

The officiant's name was Arthur McDonough, and I'd hired him after a thorough vetting on my mother's recommendation.

She was sitting in the front row of the chairs arranged in the backyard for the small circle of friends and family joining us for this event.

My mother was nervous, worried about me, but I assured her everything was going to be okay.

She knew I was telling my bosses, *my cousins,* about our familial relationship today, and she was right to be anxious.

But also, not. This was for me to deal with. Not her. I would protect my mother in all things.

"Well, that's a surprise. Though not really. You're a prick just like these two assholes," Josef muttered.

Adrik scowled at him, but Josef just shrugged unapologetically.

"Goddamn! Well, welcome to the family, Andres," Marat said, clapping me on the back.

That handsome fucker looked positively amused as he downed the rest of his drink.

"Yes, of course, welcome. But why did you not tell us this before?" Adrik asked, looking thoughtful.

"I wasn't sure I wanted you to know. You have a reputation for being, let's say, less than reasonable, and I didn't want to show my hand until I was certain I could trust you," I admitted.

"And now you can trust us?" he asked.

I nodded once.

"Now, I have to trust you, *cousin*. Today I become a husband and a father, and trusting you is how I keep my family safe."

Adrik's lips twisted into a grin, and all three men looked at me with the same expression of understanding on their faces.

They said Volkov meant *wolf*, and it was easy to see the predators staring out through their eyes.

I didn't have a plan for how I would avenge my soon-to-be wife and son.

Not exactly.

But I had backup now.

I had these men by my side, and that was good enough for me.

"Mommy!" Sammy squealed as he raced into the room and tackled me around my knees.

I was used to his exuberance and braced myself, so he didn't knock me over. He was already so strong, and not even four yet.

"You ready to do this, Bud?" I asked him, uncertainty gnawing at my insides.

"Yep! Let's get married, Mommy!"

Sofia, Destiny, and Meredith left the room, and I knew they would be lined up and waiting to precede me down the aisle. I appreciated their tact, and used those few seconds to compose myself and just look at my son.

He was dressed beautifully in a tiny little tux with a velvet bow tie that matched Andres' perfectly.

At my son's feet was Rocky. They were inseparable these days. The kitten had been outfitted with a tiny version of Sammy's bowtie and a leash.

He was even behaving properly, walking by Sammy's side, and only getting into a little bit of trouble when he sort of peed on Josef's shoe.

Andres had his tailor come over, and after a very serious discussion with Sammy, the two of them decided he would dress just like his new stepfather. And the cat would match them both.

Because it was Halloween, Sammy also wore a jet fighter backpack that looked like he had rockets tied right to his little back. And instead of a flower, he had a tiny pumpkin pinned to his lapel.

He looked adorable.

And happy.

My heart squeezed as he took my hand solemnly and started walking with me to where we'd practiced.

My stomach was in knots, but I was the one who wanted this. I was the one who'd asked Andres, a man I barely knew, to marry me.

You know what he tastes like. And that sexy growl he makes when he comes.

I closed my eyes tight and tried to shush my inner voice. I would never admit I was about to walk down the aisle with wet panties, but that was my new reality.

Seriously, I didn't know what was wrong with me.

It was like I had this secret slutty side that only emerged when I met Andres.

Our discussion the night I'd proposed to him came flooding back through my mind.

I'd been a nervous wreck, sitting across from him and trying to avoid looking at his stormy eyes. The man was seriously intense.

I mean, he'd agreed to my ridiculously inappropriate proposition almost immediately.

But Andres was a businessman—*a good one.*

He also wasn't a fool. He had stipulations.

Things I had to agree to, and I did.

Maybe a little faster than I should have.

"*S*o, *what do you want from this marriage?*" I'd asked when he brought it up.

"*I want a wife.*" Andres told me with zero humor in his stormy gaze.

"Okayyy," I replied, not seeing the problem.

"I mean, I want a real wife, Ellie. I want you in my bed."

"On our wedding night, you mean?"

"No. You will share my bed, Lupina. Starting with our wedding night and every night after."

"What?"

I remembered my shocked gasp and the way my eyes went wide. Andres' expression had somehow remained neutral, but I saw a flicker of heat.

A flash of desire in the blue-gray steel of his irises —*and it warmed me.*

"I won't take a wife who doesn't sleep beside me. What kind of life is that? What kind of example would that be for Sammy? If we are doing this, it's for keeps. Understand?"

"I understand," I said.

But I didn't. Not really. And I'd been angry.

Andres misread my anger. He continued quickly with an explanation, and I'd blushed, shaking my head.

"I don't mean that I would force you, Ellie. I would never. I swear I am not that kind of man. But I am human, very much so when it comes to you."

"I know you wouldn't force me," I said and meant it.

"You do? Good. You have to admit, Lupina, we're explosive together—"

"It was only once."

I was trying to downplay what we'd shared. I needed to dampen the sudden appetite I had for sex. Well, sex with him, if I were being honest with myself.

Truthfully, it was a hunger I'd never felt before, and it was entirely focused on him. My body buzzed with excitement when he was near. Like I was hyperaware of him on some cellular level.

I had never lusted for anyone the way I did for Andres Ramirez. He was in a class all his own.

That small, exhausted, under-used when it came to men, muscle that beat inside my chest thumped a little faster whenever he was close.

"That's right. It was only one glorious time, and I can't stop thinking about it. Can you?" he asked, licking his *bottom lip.*

He was right. I couldn't deny it.

I thought about our one time a lot. Often in the middle of the night when I could close my eyes and pretend it was him touching me, bringing me to completion.

Jesus. Christ.

He was so damn sensual. So earthy and vibrant. I

wanted to crawl on his lap and beg him for a demonstration just to prove it.

What the heck was wrong with me?

I never got like that over a man. Not ever.

Sex with Gary had been fast and humiliating.

The few times we'd actually had intercourse he'd rushed through it, and I barely knew what was happening before it was over.

After Sammy was born, Gary hardly touched me. And in the last two years, not at all.

I was ashamed to admit it, but I was glad. I didn't want his hands on me. I didn't need him telling me I was to blame for his lack of interest and second-rate performance.

Sure, for a while I blamed myself. I wasn't a virgin when I married Gary. But I'd only had sex once before him, and that too was hardly anything to write home about.

Like most first times, mine was uncomfortable and brief. We were just two virgins who thought we had to have sex after prom.

Yeah, it sucked.

Afterwards, I hadn't been in a rush to do it again. Hence the long wait from prom to marriage.

But that one night with Andres had blown my

prior, disappointing experiences right out of the water.

He'd made me feel beautiful before he even touched me. The way his eyes had raked over my body.

Hell.

I still got shivers just thinking about it. But I imagined it was just run-of-the-mill sex for a man like him.

Nothing extraordinary.

I had no misgivings about myself. I was no sex kitten.

My chubby body was okay, I mean, I wasn't ugly, and I had all the right parts. But I sincerely doubted my ability to turn a man like him on.

At least, not to the degree he was talking about.

There was no way he meant it. Why would a guy who looked like him want me like that?

"Look, you don't have to pretend this is anything other than a marriage of convenience. And I am aware it's mostly for me. I'm sure you've had other women since—"

"No one. I haven't been with another woman since I saw you."

His confession was as unexpected as my reaction to it.

Fierce, possessive need rose inside me like a tidal

wave. I had to pinch my thigh to keep from moaning out loud in satisfaction.

My mouth went dry. I didn't know what to think.

A man like him admitting he hadn't had sex in two months was astounding to me.

How could that even be possible?

"Do you really need to ask that, Lupina?" he *growled.*

I had no idea what *Lupina* meant, or why he kept calling me that. But more importantly, I had no answer for him.

I mean, yeah, I really needed to ask.

"Okay, so you want us to sleep together. Is what you are saying?" I finally asked bluntly.

"Yes. I want a real marriage. I won't settle for less than real with you."

"Why aren't you already married? Oh my God, do you have a girlfriend?"

"Ellie, why would I agree to marry you if I had a girl-friend? And I just told you I haven't slept with anyone since I first saw you."

"Right," I whispered.

"I don't lie. I won't lie. Not to you. Not about us. It will always only be the truth between you and me, okay? No secrets. No lies."

I wanted to believe him so badly. Trust was difficult for me. But Andres had only ever been kind, and I had no reason to doubt him.

I didn't believe in making one person pay for the sins of another. Andres wasn't Gary. That was a mistake I could never make.

So, once more, I'd agreed to his terms.

"Okay, so we get married. We sleep together. We make this real. No lying. And no cheating."

"No cheating?"

"You can't sleep with other women, Andres. I can't open myself up to that kind of—"

"I will never touch another woman. I swear it. And you won't touch another man."

He'd said it with a finality I would never admit out loud to liking, but I did.

I liked it a lot.

There was just something so freeing in his statement. There were a few other things he asked for, things having to do with my inheritance and the business, and I agreed to all of them.

I didn't know much about it to be honest, but Andres had me meet with his lawyers the next day. He insisted I have representation of my own, and I called one of my Dad's old friends who ran a law firm.

After an hour of legal jargon, I distracted myself

with some reading until my lawyer told me everything looked fantastic and that I should sign on the dotted line to whatever agreement Andres had drawn up.

So, I did.

It was insane, but I completely trusted Andres to do right by me and Sammy. I couldn't explain it. I just knew instinctively that he wouldn't hurt us like that.

Where I got that knowledge after my disastrous first marriage, I had no idea.

But my therapist said I needed to learn to trust again, and I had to start somewhere.

So, I was starting with myself.

Which was exactly how I wound up getting married to an almost stranger on Halloween in one of my new best friends' backyards.

I couldn't see Andres yet. And the waiting was making me tense.

Sammy swung our hands back and forth, and I spared a glance for my little boy.

He was grinning widely, but the second the music started, he got all serious.

My heart squeezed as I watched him take his first step very carefully, just like we practiced.

I'd wanted Sammy to be a part of the ceremony

as much as possible, and when Andres suggested he be the one to walk me down the aisle, I almost cried.

It was perfect.

I scanned the dozen guests gathered to celebrate with us and nodded nervously. My gaze stopped on a smallish woman whose coloring was too much like Andres' to be anyone other than his mother.

She smiled kindly at me and lowered her gaze to Sammy's. He looked at me, then back at her, a shy grin on his face before he waved at her.

I swallowed the lump in my throat. Sammy had no memories of my father, and Gary's parents had long since passed.

My son had no living grandparents. Until now.

My eyes flicked up to Andres in that moment, and everything else just seemed to fall away.

He was breathtaking in his tuxedo, his velvet tie matching Sammy's. He'd trimmed his beard and hair, and I found it suddenly very warm.

He was unerringly groomed, showing off his chiseled features.

He was so—*so much.*

So thoughtful.

He planned the entire wedding. Thought of the theme, the clothes, the food, the music, everything.

So practical.

He made it easy to move into his condo. Set up everything with the lawyers so it would be legit. Really, I had to do nothing but simply exist.

So giving.

I mean, he was literally giving up his freedom to help me.

And he was so goddamn handsome.

So gracefully masculine.

I was powerless to do anything but stare at him as I slow-walked down the aisle.

But then I noticed his expression.

Stony. Firm. Almost scary.

Not like I was scared for my life kind of scary, but he was just so serious.

Unsmiling. Intense. Ferocious.

Like a predator stalking his prey.

Granted, we weren't a love match. I knew that. I wasn't delusional or anything. But I thought maybe he would smile at me.

If it wasn't for Sammy's little hand tugging me along, I doubted I would have moved at all.

Somehow, I managed. I put one foot after the other and marched towards my future with my head high and my eyes wide open.

We were really doing this.

Holy. *Shit.*

We were really doing this.

The second Ellie agreed to my demands, I put this whole thing into motion. I planned everything. The whole wedding.

Yeah, Ellie had a say, but she seemed content to just say *I do* in a courthouse.

Not me. I knew this was the only time I was ever getting married. I didn't want to run away and elope. I wanted to celebrate it.

To celebrate her.

Maybe it was backwards to start out this way. But Ellie Maxwell, *soon to be Ramirez,* was mine.

From the second I saw her, I'd claimed her. Even if only in my mind.

I knew Ellie Maxwell was made for me.

The one time I made love to her was stamped inside my brain. That experience was unforgettable.

Yeah, I claimed Ellie with my body. And I couldn't fucking wait to do it again.

But first, right now, before our friends and family, I was going to claim her with words. Announcing my vow to her, promising before God and the whole fucking universe that this woman was mine.

She is mine.

And I meant to keep her.

Okay, so I was a little fucking obsessed.

But this was something I wanted so damn badly, I could taste it. All my life, I'd had to work for what I wanted.

And I was willing to work to get Ellie.

Marrying her was just another step in my plan. Because I didn't only want her to wear my ring on her finger. I wanted it wrapped around her heart.

I wanted to fill her mind, to encompass her thoughts, the way she filled mine day in and day out.

I wanted to pleasure her body every fucking night. To fill her with my seed. To make her come like no one else ever had.

I wanted to imprint myself on her very fucking soul.

When Ellie was around, everything else was second. She had all my attention. All my focus.

But I knew she needed me to tone it down. It wasn't like I could just tell her I was borderline fucking nuts when it came to her.

She had no idea the things I would do. The blood I would spill. The bridges I'd burn. And the lives I would fucking shatter all for the sake of her and Sammy.

To keep them safe, I'd push all kinds of boundaries. There wasn't a damn thing I'd consider too much or too far. Not for them.

But being around her the last couple of days and not touching her? That was fucking rough. More than that. It was hell.

Pure. Hell.

"Easy, cousin. She's coming," Adrik murmured, and I exhaled.

He was right. I needed to take it easy. After the stress of the last few days, that was easier said than done.

Lucky for me, I had a wedding to plan, her father's business to vet, and her piece of shit ex to fuck with to keep me busy.

The wedding planning was surprisingly fun. Knowing how she loved Halloween above all other holidays, I planned our big day around it.

I'd heard her say it at one of the *Sourdough Sunday* lunches Adrik had hosted at his and Sofia's place.

So, I sent her a bunch of gowns to choose from, hired the best event planner, and asked Meredith and Josef to host.

I even had my tailor make Sammy a tux that matched mine, except for the rocket backpack, which, looking at it now, might have made a cool addition to my getup.

Hundreds of Gerbera daisies with dark, leafy green accents and mossy fronds, also Ellie's favorite, decorated the chairs and the espresso-stained wooden arch where I waited for her.

My mom smiled at me with tears in her eyes. They were the same blue-gray as mine. I knew she worried about me, and I hoped this would settle some of her fears.

I'd expected more of an objection from her since she'd never even met my bride, but she trusted me to make good decisions. Plus, the prospect of having a built-in grandson was just icing on the cake.

"Oh! I'm gonna ask him to call me Nana, think that'll be okay?" she asked when I told her.

"I think it will be great, Mom. Thank you."

"For what?" she asked.

"For being amazing and accepting all this," I told her honestly.

"Andy boy, I trust you to know what you're doing. Now, tell me about my new grandson!"

I glanced down at Sammy, offering a proud smile to the boy who was about to become *my boy*.

Pride filled me, and another emotion so strong, I had to blink to stop it rolling down my face.

It felt like I was born to be that child's father.

He smiled back, and the tightness around my heart eased. I winked, then I lifted my gaze.

Slowly.

I knew she would be beautiful.

Had thought so the first time I laid eyes on her.

But seeing sweet Ellie Maxwell draped in layer after layer of sheer black lace was more than I'd ever hoped for.

Her pale skin practically glowed in that dress. Her hair was a little longer now, almost touching her pretty shoulders in glossy curls.

The sides and front were pinned back in some complicated twist, and she had a flower in her hair.

Fuck.

She looked amazing.

The perfect blend of innocent and decadent. Black lace and sheer layers of fabric wrapped around her lovingly. Casting shadows as she walked, I hummed appreciatively as hints of soft, pale skin flashed with every move my sweet Lupina made.

Goddamn.

She was stunning, Just like I knew she would be.

Other girls might be right for pristine white and red roses. But Ellie was different.

She was special.

A cut apart from the rest. A veritable goddess decked out in midnight colored fabric.

Ellie was mine. And that was all that mattered.

I held my hand out towards her, waiting for the moment her skin touched mine.

Ellie bent down first, kissing Sammy on the cheek. Then she straightened her back and faced me.

Powerful, courageous, warrior woman. My woman.

Next, she placed her soft hand in mine, and I felt the triumph of it sing through my soul.

"Dearly beloved," Deacon McDonough began.

"Look this way please," the photographer said, and I turned my attention towards the smiling woman.

I couldn't believe it happened so quickly. But the ceremony was over, and I was now Mrs. Ellie Ramirez.

Holy. Shit

We'd decided on a light fare with Autumn themed cocktails and appetizers passed out by servers after the ceremony.

We already cut the cake, and coffee was now being served in pretty little demitasse cups.

It was a delicious confection made of dark chocolate and the most sublime buttercream on the whole planet, decked out with realistic replicas of my bouquet made out of spun sugar.

I looked down at the beautiful princess cut black diamond surrounded by dozens of sparkling baguettes in a platinum setting sitting on my finger, and my eyes widened.

He'd nailed it. There was something about the stone that just drew me. Maybe it was the mystery behind it. Or the fact black was not the normal color for a wedding dress or ring.

But I always liked it. My fascination with Halloween started when I was a child and I wanted to wear a scary witch costume.

My nanny insisted on me wearing a princess dress. I caved.

Of course I did.

I'd wanted to be liked and loved, and my father cared, but he was never one to coddle. So I did what I was told.

I always did what I was told. But I didn't want to. Not anymore.

Andres really had thought of everything.

The ring.

The dress.

The party.

Everything.

He did everything. Things I hadn't even asked him to see to. Things I was hardly willing to admit I wanted.

I didn't know how to handle it. I mean this was a marriage of convenience.

Mainly mine.

But Andres made it seem like more. Like this was something he actually wanted and not something I just threw out at him in a moment of desperation.

"Coffee?" he asked, coming towards me with an espresso in his hand.

"Is it spiked?" I asked.

"Just a little," Andres said, his lips quirked up in a rare teasing grin.

He held the cup to my lips, and my pulse raced.

It was nothing, really.

Just my new husband sharing his coffee with me.

Nothing to write home about.

But my hand trembled as I touched his, allowing him to tilt the delicate ceramic so I could swallow the delicious dark brew.

"Good?" he asked once I'd taken a small sip, relishing the licorice-flavored liquor he'd added to it.

"Mm hm. Sambuca?"

"Anisette," he corrected me.

I hummed again, and Andres grinned. My lips parted.

Christ, he was good looking.

He downed the rest of the coffee in a single gulp. I watched his throat work and heat flooded my system.

Why was that sexy?

He was just a man drinking espresso, for God's sake. Not like he was one of those shirtless lumberjacks that kept popping up on my social media feed.

Don't ask.

Again, I reminded myself it was no big deal.

But that was a lie. I was fooling myself.

It was something. The simple act of sharing coffee was monumental somehow. I felt my pulse quicken and my heart squeeze.

Maybe it was the intimacy of it that left me a little breathless.

"Did you see Sammy before he went to bed?" I asked, knowing how Andres enjoyed tucking him in.

"I did. I must have just missed you. I gave him a kiss goodnight after he'd already fallen asleep," he said with a shrug.

I smiled indulgently. My son was my pride and joy, and it was one subject Andres and I seemed to have no trouble communicating about at all.

Was it wrong that I loved how openly affectionate he was with Sammy?

Andres didn't shy from hugs or sticky kisses. Sammy was still young enough to enjoy being petted and praised. And Andres indulged him with genuine affection.

He never had anything like that from Gary. I was worried he would be afraid, living with a man after months of it being just us. But he wasn't.

Maybe it was because Sammy and Andres had formed a bond over the past few months. We'd seen him at every Sourdough Saturday and at other times when we visited Meredith or one of the other women.

Andres was good to my son. And that made me like him a little more than I should.

Sammy deserved to be happy and safe. I just needed to remind myself that was the reason for our marriage.

We got married to protect Sammy from Gary. Not because we were in love or anything.

Why did that make my heart hurt?

"He must have conked out right away, huh?"

"Oh, yeah. Poor little guy was all tuckered out. I mean, after all this excitement, who wouldn't be?" I shrugged.

"What do you mean? The party?"

"Well, Sammy just got a new stepdad and a new grandmother. He was thrilled when she asked him to call her Nana," I told Andres, waiting for him to gift me with one of his rare smiles.

He did, and I almost swooned at his feet.

I had to admit I'd been nervous about meeting her, but Andres' mom was fantastic. A sweet, wonderful woman who obviously loved her son.

"Oh, that reminds me, the car is here to take my mother back to her place in Hoboken. But I know she'd like to say goodbye to you, if you don't mind."

"Um, sure," I agreed, closing my eyes for a second when I felt his hand on the small of my back.

Andres had been touching me all night.

Not blatantly. Not in any way that would make anyone notice.

But I noticed.

It was like every brush of his fingers across my body was him marking me in some way, branding me as his. I nodded my head, allowing him to gently guide me to the front door where his mother, who insisted I call her Nancy, was waiting.

"There she is. My beautiful new daughter! Now, I know you're both leaving for this one night honeymoon of yours, and you have loads to do to get settled in, but I want you to come visit soon with my baby boy," Nancy said.

"Mom, I'm thirty-seven," Andres teased his mother.

"Not you! I meant my little Sammy. Anyway, I just wanted to say, Ellie, I am so happy my Andres found such a special woman to share his life with. He works so hard—"

"Mom," Andres moaned.

"Okay, okay. Congratulations again, my darlings," she said, squeezing both of our hands and tugging us forward for cheek kisses.

"Thank you. It was so nice to meet you," I replied, a little embarrassed.

"I'll walk you out, Mom. Be right back."

Andres' hand contracted on my back as he stepped away from me to walk his mother to the car. I bit my lip and watched him.

"That's a good man right there, taking care of his mom like that," Meredith whispered from right beside me, and I jumped.

"Christ, Meredith! Are you trying to give me a heart attack?"

"Uh no. I'm just saying, Andres is a really good guy. I mean, look how gorgeous everything was tonight. He went above and beyond—"

"He hired a planner. It's not that big a deal," I muttered, refusing to acknowledge what she was trying to do.

"Um, actually, he sent a ten paragraph email to the planner detailing everything from the menu to the flowers to the lighting. If I'm not mistaken, Andres is meticulous like that in every aspect of his life, but you would know better than me," she said, waggling her eyebrows at me.

I shook my head, biting my lip to stifle my giggle.

She wasn't wrong.

Andres was a generous man.

In all ways.

My body heated, and my mouth was dry. I licked my lips, watching as he closed the door after his mother got inside the car.

Andres tapped the roof, signaling to the driver, and he backed up a step to watch the vehicle pulling away until it turned around the corner.

He really was a good man. And it dawned on me right then, Andres was my man.

My husband.

Technically, it wasn't wrong for me to want him in that way. It didn't make me depraved or sick to imagine his hands on my body or his lips crushing mine.

Sammy was safe and secure. Josef was the motherfucking head of security for Volkov Industries, and he ran his own very successful, very lethal, security firm. My son wouldn't be safer if he were in Fort Knox.

I'd already had my fill of food and drink and conversation. In fact, I felt more myself tonight than I had in years.

There was one common denominator in all of it. And that was Andres.

Maybe I was moving too fast.

Maybe I should work harder to separate the reasons we married.

I was tired of ignoring the way my chest tightened and my pulse reacted whenever his stormy eyes met mine.

Maybe I should have fought harder against his insistence that we make this thing real.

But even if I had, even if this was all a mistake, it didn't change how I felt right then.

Warm. Needy. Wet.

Tonight I was a newly married woman, and I wanted my husband with a hunger I'd never felt.

Suddenly, I was very ready to leave.

CHAPTER TWELVE ANDRES

I walked into the condo after my wife.

Fuck.

Heat filled me. Ellie was finally mine.

My wife.

Just the thought had my cock hardening behind my pants.

I watched the layers of her skirt swirl around her calves, and goddamn I swear I felt the entire world shift on its axis.

I told Ellie I wanted a wedding night.

A real one.

I wanted this marriage to be real, and that included a mature, consensual, sexual relationship.

And she agreed.

She fucking agreed.

I'd been waiting for that moment all night long. I craved her touch. Needed to feel her writhing beneath me.

From the second I saw her walking towards me down the aisle, across the black carpet that glittered with hundreds of sparkles sewn across it, making it look like she was floating across a piece of the night sky, I wanted her with a fierce hunger I could barely comprehend.

For months, I'd watched Ellie from afar. I'd wondered about who she really was, what she was running from.

I'd been inexplicably drawn to the woman with the mischievous light dancing behind her gold-green eyes from the first second I saw her.

But I never imagined she'd ask me to marry her. Even if it wasn't for the usual reasons.

Love could come later.

But the moment she'd said *I do,* there was no going back. Not for me. Not for her.

Ellie was going to be mine forever.

Obsessive much?

Fuck yes.

I stretched my neck, my hungry gaze eating up every inch of her as she drew closer.

Ever since the wedding march hummed from the

small quartet, playing unobtrusively from beneath an arch decked out with flowers and ribbons, I'd been revved up like an engine idling just waiting for permission to blast off.

It was still something I needed to process, that I was a married man. That I was married to the woman who consumed my every thought.

The wedding itself went without a hitch. The event planner had outdone herself. It was everything I'd imagined.

I paid well, so it was to be expected. But seeing the delight on Ellie's face as she'd taken in every detail had been worth all my meticulous planning, the emails, and lists of things I'd wanted for tonight.

Getting married on October 31st warranted a little something extra. Getting married to Ellie demanded it.

My mother had been uncertain about the whole Halloween thing, but honestly, I couldn't have been happier with the results.

The wedding theme was perfect. Ellie was perfect. Dressed in black like the sultry seductress she was. Hell. I couldn't take my eyes off her the whole night.

Never had I encountered a woman so damn

mysterious, so alluring. I wanted to learn all her secrets. To discover every inch of her myself.

It was like she wore a mask every day of her life. Like she was hiding something from the public.

Something so dark and secret, so utterly wild, that whoever had witnessed it before had told her to hide it.

I would never do that to her.

Never.

I craved Ellie's wild side. I wanted to see it. To learn every secret and dream. Everything she yearned for.

And I wanted to be the one to give it to her.

Desire roared to life like a hungry beast, gnawing at my insides.

Fuck, I need this woman.

She was mine now, and that meant every single part of her was mine, too.

Her steps slowed as she turned to face me, and I froze, watching her like a wolf eyed his next meal.

All of Manhattan glittered behind her like a billion dollar backdrop, but my gaze was riveted to my bride.

"So, what now?" she whispered the question.

Ellie held me captive with her golden green eyes riveted to mine.

All my attention was on her, for her, and that was dangerous.

For both of us.

I'd seen men obsessed with their women. And it wasn't always pretty.

Take the dangerous men I worked for.

I knew the things they'd done to keep their wives. And I knew the things I was willing to do for mine.

That was my fate now.

I was not just a man trying to leave his mark on the world. Not some poor kid from Hoboken looking to make bank. I was a husband. A father. Protector.

And a lover.

"Now, we make this legal," I replied, lifting my hand to flash the platinum band I would never take off.

"Now we make this legal," she repeated.

Ellie licked her lips. Her chest rose and fell rapidly with her increased breathing.

Why so nervous, Lupina?

She wasn't afraid of me. I knew she wasn't. We'd been together intimately once before.

I knew she knew I wouldn't hurt her.

No, her reticence was from something else. A

sliver of self-doubt, perhaps. Or a memory of something her fucking prick of an ex said or did.

Fury filled me for an instant, but I pushed it away.

That prick would get what was coming to him. And I'd be the one to deliver it.

But those dark thoughts were for another time.

I took off my jacket and pulled on my bow tie, loosening it. Ellie followed suit, kicking off her low heels.

"Can you?" she asked, turning away from me, and offering me a view of the dozens of tiny buttons down her back.

"Yeah," I whispered, and squeezed my hands together to stop them from shaking.

I was smoother than that, for fuck's sake.

My heart was pounding as I worked those buttons free, revealing her smooth, soft, pale skin as I went.

The flash of something around her waist caught my eye, and I bit back my groan.

A garter belt.

She was wearing a fucking garter belt.

I forced myself to step back. My eyes bored into her flesh, trying to imprint that moment on my brain.

As if I could forget how she looked. My Lupina. Sweetness and sin wrapped up in silky black lace.

"Turn around," I commanded.

She did. Holding her dress to her chest.

"Take it off, Lupina. Show me."

She swallowed and nodded, holding the gown to her breasts while tugging off her sleeves one at a time.

Then, all of a sudden, she let go.

And I forgot how to breathe.

Holy. Fuck.

My nerves went off the charts as I stood before my new husband in the naughty bit of silk and lace Meredith had given me as a wedding gift.

I couldn't wear a bra beneath my dress. It had built-in cups. But the black lace thong and garter belt, complete with silk, thigh high stockings were something else.

I'd been worried they'd dig into my thick thighs or roll down halfway. But these seemed made for women like me.

Bigger women with meat on their bones.

I'd worried maybe this was too much. Like maybe it was foolish to assume he wanted to have sex with me on our wedding night.

Even though he already told me he did want that.

He wanted me.

I could see it in his stormy gaze. Appreciation for my curves, lust glittering in his irises.

I just couldn't wrap my head around it.

I mean why would someone as sinfully sexy as Andres Ramirez want me? Almost every time I'd seen him, I'd been frumpy.

What mother of a preschool aged son wouldn't be?

Usually dressed in jeans and t-shirts, I did my best to be clean, but fashion wasn't something I worried about much anymore. I didn't have to be stylish to take care of Sammy.

Andres was very stylish, though. He was always wearing tailored slacks and button downs or fitted polo shirts. His hard body was evident beneath the expensive clothes he wore.

Like the other husbands, he wore suits almost every day. I supposed it was for work, but goddamn, he always looked so good.

This was the first time I felt like his equal in that arena. Not that he ever complained or said anything about how I dressed.

My assets were all tied up in court, so I couldn't

afford to go shopping even if I wanted to. But right then, I didn't feel like anything less.

I felt desired.

Wanted.

And that was something new. I wasn't down on myself, but I was a realist. I had a mirror, and I knew what my body looked like.

But it was more than obvious Andres liked what he saw.

Watching him stare at me as I stood there practically naked, like I was something beautiful and worthy of his desire, was amazing.

Suddenly, I lost my inhibitions.

I took a step towards him, watching the rise and fall of his chest. How it increased with every step I took.

Just like mine.

Emboldened, I continued. Letting him look his fill at my imperfections, and owning every jiggle and bounce of my soft flesh I knew was on display.

I didn't stop until I was right in front of him, almost touching, but not quite.

"Ellie," he growled my name.

Andres' eyes stayed locked on mine for a beat before dropping to take in every inch of my curvy frame. I sucked in a breath, and it was enough to cause my bare breasts to brush against the fabric of his shirt.

The sensation had a gasp leaving my mouth before I could stop it.

That sound was the whistle Andres was waiting for to make his move. And it was just what I needed him to do.

Big, warm hands reached for me. At the same time, he lowered his head, claiming my lips in a kiss that was nothing like the chaste peck he gave me in front of our friends and his mother earlier in the evening when we said our *I dos*.

"Ellie," he growled again, saying my name into my mouth, his tongue chasing the words until it was dueling with mine.

I moaned, opening for him as I pressed my body to his. He was so hard and warm. So goddamn sexy in his black tux.

His hands squeezed my hips before moving lower to grab my ass. Then he was pulling me closer, one hand diving between my legs from the back, cupping my hot, needy pussy.

Andres' chest rumbled, and he lifted me up just like that. One hand squeezing my cheek, the other between my legs.

I gasped, holding onto his shoulders. Then I

wrapped my legs around his waist, pressing my core against him.

"Fuck. You're fucking soaked," he grunted.

His long fingers were stroking me over the lacy material of my thong as he walked us towards the bedroom.

I'd spent the last couple of days sleeping in the guest bedroom down the hall from his, but all my belongings had been moved the day before.

I knew I'd be sleeping in there with him after the ceremony, but it was still a shock to see my perfume, my hairbrush, my bag of makeup, and other knickknacks on the dresser and lining the shelves.

It should have looked odd, all my feminine clutter inside the utterly masculine space. But it didn't. It looked right somehow.

I landed on the bed with a little bounce and licked my lips as Andres tore off his shirt and stepped out of his pants. His tented black silk boxers made my fingers itch to touch him.

To touch it.

And I surprised myself, going up on my knees and stretching out my hand to do just that.

"Fuck, that's it. Touch me, Angel. Feel how hard I am for you? That's all for you. All yours," he groaned, crawling up onto the mattress and forcing me to back up before he ran me over.

Not that I'd mind at the moment.

His cock pulsed beneath my searching hand, the silky fabric of his boxers slid up and down as I traced him.

I pulled them down, needing to feel his velvet-covered steel in my grip with no barriers between us.

My pussy contracted on air, arousal spilling down my thighs. I was so fucking hot for this man. Needed him so badly.

"Goddamn, Lupina. So fucking perfect. Lay back. Spread your legs."

"W-why?"

"Cause I want to taste what's mine," he growled, and my eyes rolled back.

I was panting with need at that point, and my body obeyed his command.

I leaned back, not caring about my belly rolls or the way my thighs jiggled when I spread my legs for him.

"So fucking perfect," Andres growled.

He tugged my thong to the side, revealing my slick sex to his searching gaze. I covered my eyes. Then I dropped my hands.

I wanted to watch him. To see his expression when he tasted me.

Fuck. It felt so naughty to want those things.

But sometimes naughty was nice, right?

"You're dripping, Lupina," he moaned.

He actually frigging moaned.

Like I was one of those triple decker chocolate fudge brownies the café on the corner served. I only knew they were good because Meredith's husband was forever plying her with those decadent desserts.

His head dipped down, bringing him closer, ever closer, to where I needed him. But he stopped just short of the mark.

"Andres," I moaned, flexing my hips.

"So needy, Wife. Don't worry. I'll take care of you. I will always take care of you, Lupina," he growled before he pounced.

Holy. Fuck.

Andres closed his hot mouth over my pussy, sucking my clit inside his wet warmth, and I moaned.

Sensation after sensation slammed into me one by one, like a freight train going off the rails.

Pleasure built upon pleasure, colliding into me with such force, my legs shook.

I'd never had a man do what he was doing to me. Eating me with such fervent desire.

"Keep your legs wide," he commanded, and I fought against the urge to squeeze them shut.

Andres hummed against my sex, his tongue laving at me, and I almost imploded. His sensual assault was relentless, delicious, and fervent.

I had no choice but to hold on and take it.

And I did.

My hands clutched at his short hair, and I lifted my hips, flexing against his mouth, working my body into a frenzy.

"That's it, Lupina. Take your pleasure from me," he murmured, making his tongue stiff but not moving.

"Andres," I moaned, needing more.

Andres lifted his face, his stormy eyes blazing with lust.

"Do it. Fuck my face, and make yourself come," he growled.

Then he did it again.

Andres made his tongue hard and tight against my clit, one big hand circled my hip holding me tight to him while he speared my pussy with two thick fingers.

I was mindless with need. But I knew what he

wanted me to do. And I wanted it, too.

Heat.

So much of it. Dark, dirty, wet heat filled me.

Fueling my desire.

I reached for him, holding his head as I flexed my hips.

Chasing my orgasm, I rocked my core against his face, rubbing my clit on his tongue and loving every second of it.

I couldn't believe I was really doing that.

That I, Ellie Maxwell, the last person in the world to incite passion in a man, was doing just as my new husband demanded.

Even more unbelievable, I felt incredible.

Powerful. In control. Strong. And sexy.

I never thought I could let go with someone like that.

But I did.

With him.

A long, keening moan spilled from my lips as I fucked my husband's face.

He was everywhere. He was everything.

Lapping at my cunt. Praising me with his moans. Making me squirm and writhe like a wanton thing.

I came apart harder than ever before.

Sharp shards of pleasure sliced through me, pleasure so powerful it was on the brink of pain, and I knew this was something phenomenal.

This surely wasn't normal. My reaction to him was not normal.

How could I feel so good because of one person's attentions?

Never. I never experienced anything like it.

I'd never been the focus of one man's mission to deliver physical pleasure.

It was foreign. Filthy. And so fucking good.

He made me feel so good.

It was even a little scary, because even though I just came harder than ever before, I wanted to feel it again.

Right now. With him.

I wanted my husband to fuck me. I needed his cock inside me, filling me.

And I was ready to demand it.

Ellie was spread out across our bed like a carnal banquet, and my mouth watered.

So fucking delicious.

Eating her out was about to make me come in my boxers like a goddamn teenager.

Not doing more than holding my position was fucking killing me, but I needed her to know she was good at this.

I needed her to know she had me, for better or worse. And she could fucking take me anytime she wanted.

See, to me, confidence was the sexiest goddamn thing a woman could wear.

My Ellie might have had some hard knocks, but

beneath the painful memories, she was a fucking she-Wolf.

My Lupina.

A fierce motherfucking warrior of a woman who would put herself in danger to protect her son, who had the courage to leave a situation the second it got out of hand.

She was phenomenal. And I wanted her to know it. I fucking needed her to.

Really, I wasn't complaining. Drinking Ellie's pleasure from the source was better than I even imagined.

I wanted to stay with my face buried between her thighs for the rest of my fucking life. But my aching cock demanded more.

Feeling her pussy ripple around my fingers and my tongue was like fucking nirvana. I indulged myself with one more long lick from her tight rosebud to her hard little clit.

Goddamn.

I was wild for her.

So hot. So dirty. So good.

She came once, but I wasn't through with her. Not by a long shot.

Tonight, once wasn't enough.

"Ready for me, Wife?"

I had to ask. I was thick and long, and I needed her ready to take me. I was too far gone for slow or gentle lovemaking.

Nah. That wasn't going to work for me.

I needed to fuck my wife. To feel her slippery cunt suck the cum right out of my body.

"Ready to take this dick?"

Her luminous eyes were lust glazed as she nodded her head.

So fucking hot.

Her musky sweet flavors danced across my taste buds as I licked my lips, and I was more than ready to take what was mine.

I slid up her body, memorizing every inch of her as I went. Every dip and curve. Every dimple and freckle.

Goddamn.

She was so fucking soft. Her skin was so warm and pink with desire. I never wanted anyone like I wanted her.

Ellie was perfect.

"Gonna fuck you now, Angel. Gonna make you come on my cock," I said, waiting for her to nod again before I moved.

My cock was dripping with precum. I couldn't wait to push between her hot, slick folds. But I did.

"Please," she begged, and fuck, that was my undoing.

I would never make her wait.

Not when she wanted me as badly as I wanted her.

"Fucking perfect," I grunted and pressed forward, losing myself to the sensation of being inside my sweet wife.

Heat.

Wet, pulsating heat wrapped around me, and I fucking lost all track of time as I seated myself deep within her body.

"Christ, you're so tight. Need you naked, Angel. Need all your soft skin touching me," I grunted.

Her tight cunt pulsed around me.

Fuck.

She liked that.

She liked knowing I needed her.

That was good. I didn't think I'd ever stop needing her.

I groaned as I pushed us further up the bed. I needed her closer. I needed more.

I took her sexy underwear and garters in my grip, and I pulled, tearing them off. I tossed them aside as I rolled the stockings down her legs, helping her kick those off too.

Then I ghosted my hands up her legs, her hips, her belly, her fucking tits. Goddamn. I wanted to touch every inch of her. To lay claim to her.

That Ellie was an active participant, moving to help me, and using her feet to push my boxers all the way off, was icing on the fucking cake.

"Andres," she moaned my name, raking her nails down my back, and my whole body shivered with need.

My cock was ready to burst the second I slid inside her, but I couldn't just bust my nut and leave her unsatisfied.

Not tonight. Not ever.

No fucking way.

"I've been dying to get back inside your tight cunt ever since that first night," I said.

"Please," she begged again.

"You're so wet for me, Lupina. You been thinking about this too, right? Thinking about how I fucked you on that sofa. You were so fucking hot and soaked for me. That's it, squeeze me with your cunt. Let me feel how much you want me."

"I do! I want you so bad," she whispered, and it was the best damn thing I ever heard.

I kept whispering, kept talking, holding myself

still while I told her all the dirty things going through my mind.

I licked a trail from her mouth to her tits, tonguing her cleavage before sucking one tight bud into my mouth.

"These tits are so fucking perfect. They fit right inside my mouth. You love it when I suck them, don't you? You love my mouth on your body. Tell me."

"Andres," she whimpered.

I couldn't take it anymore, finally, I started moving my hips.

Ellie moaned, her small hands clutching at my shoulders while I slid my cock almost all the way out until just the tip sat inside her clenching walls.

"Tell me you love it when I fuck you," I demanded.

"I do. I love it when you fuck me. I love your mouth on my body," she said, finally repeating what I needed to hear.

Ellie scratched at my shoulders, her cunt tightening around the tip of my dick, but I held still.

She whimpered next, and I pressed in a little more, dragging that sound from her lips again.

Fuck. I fucking love hearing her whimper.

"What else do you love, huh? You love it when I tongue fuck this cunt, Wife?"

"Y-yes. I loved it," she moaned, and I slipped another inch inside her.

"And my dick? You love my dick when I'm buried balls deep inside your soaked little slit?"

"Yes! Yes! Andres please," she pleaded, gasping as I withdrew again.

"Not Andres. Call me something else."

"What?"

"Who am I?"

"Y-you're Andres," she frowned, trying to flex her hips, enticing me to pound into her hot as fuck sex.

"What am I, *Lupina*? Who am I, *Wife*?" I asked again, my growl positively feral.

Her hazel eyes flashed at me. The amber and green swirls were more pronounced in her lust-glazed stare as she finally understood what I wanted.

"You're my, my husband. My Andres. Please, Husband," she begged again, sobbing with need.

Pleasure roared in my veins, and I slammed home, going as deep as possible and grinding against her clit.

My husband.

Fuck.

Yes.

I shoved my dick so far inside her, I was almost sure she could fucking taste it.

An image of Ellie on her knees with my cock down her throat flashed through my mind, and I groaned, crashing my lips to hers as I fucked her harder and faster.

"You're so fucking good. Open up for me. Take every inch. Take it all, Wife."

I licked into her mouth one more time before moving to my knees, needing the leverage, wanting to see her tits bounce as I pounded into her.

My hands gripped her hips, lifting and tilting her so she was practically sitting on my thighs.

"Are you close, Wife? Are you gonna come all over my cock?"

"Y-yes. Yes, Husband. I'm so close."

Good. I needed her close. I needed her to fucking explode just like I was going to.

"Touch your clit, Angel. Rub that little bud and come all over my dick. I want your pleasure dripping down my balls," I told her.

"Oh God, so close," she moaned.

I knew the language I was using was rough and raw and she wasn't used to it. But she liked it. I could tell by the way her cunt squeezed me so good with every syllable I uttered.

"Tell me when you come. I want to hear it," I demanded.

Flexing my hips, I pressed the base of my cock against her clit. Grinding into that tiny little nubbin with precise circular motions.

Swivel. Grind. Flex. Pump.

"Oh yes. Husband, I'm coming. I'm coming!" she shouted.

"That's it, Wife. Come harder. Keep rubbing that clit till you suck the cum right outta my dick. Fuck, yes, feel me filling you up," I growled, slamming all the way in.

I threw my head back as a rush of pure fucking pleasure coursed through my veins. Ellie's hands caught my hips, squeezing as she continued to come.

"Holy fuck, that was," she whispered eons later when we were both still trying to catch our breath.

"Yeah. It was," I replied with a grin.

"Andres, I never felt like that. I mean, that was—" she sputtered.

I leaned back, my half-hard cock was still buried inside of her.

"Never? Good. Gimme a few minutes, Wife, and I'll fuck you like that again."

Her cunt squeezed me, and I moaned.

My dick turned to steel, and I rocked my hips.

She moaned with me that time.

"Who needs a few minutes?" I muttered.

"You can't be ready again? That's not possible," she said, eyes wide as saucers.

"Not possible? Lupina, I'm so fucking hard for you. Gonna stay buried in this pussy right here all fucking night. That okay with you, Wife?"

She blinked. Licked her lips. Then she nodded.

"Yeah. That's okay with me."

I grinned.

I knew Ellie and I were going to be explosive in bed. From the first time I saw her, I had an inkling.

Sure, I wanted more than just sex from her.

I wanted everything.

I wanted her heart.

Her love.

Her loyalty.

But I had to start somewhere. Getting her addicted to my cock was as good a place as any.

Her moans and pants were like music to my ears, and I couldn't wait to memorize every inch of her hot little body.

She was sensual and earthy, and it was clear to me whoever she'd been with before had neglected that side of her.

Not that I wanted to think about her having sex

with anyone else. As far as I was concerned, my wife was a fucking virgin until me.

I know, I know it was a total dickhead thing to think. But what could I say?

From the things we did together, and her reactions to my sensual overtures, it was obvious her past lovers hadn't been attentive. Hell, Ellie might as well have been a virgin.

I didn't know whether to pound my chest and roar that I was the one to teach her real pleasure. Or to hunt down the assholes who didn't provide her with what she deserved.

Maybe I would do both.

I knew men who blamed incompatibility or laziness in bed on the women. But that was bullshit. Sex was natural, and it should be good for everyone involved or not done.

Ellie wasn't frigid or cold or whatever it was her asshole ex had tried to convince her while placing the blame of his inferior performance on her.

Truth was my wife was fire. She was a dirty little girl.

Seductive. Tempting. Responsive. And so fucking real.

I fucking loved it.

I loved everything about being with her.

I love her.

"So, how's married life?"

I looked up from the dough I'd been kneading and met three pairs of curious and amused eyes.

Thanksgiving was one week away, and Sofia had invited everyone over to test out some recipes for the holiday festivities.

She was hosting. And we were all invited.

"Um, good," I replied.

Honestly, it was good. Andres was like the perfect man.

He was attentive. Yet he gave me space. He was wonderful with Sammy. And at night, he loved me with a fervor I'd never experienced.

But I felt something lacking between us.

It was stupid.

I was being stupid.

I mean, we weren't a love match. But there was something about his demeanor that made me wish we were.

Christ, I was losing it.

I couldn't help it. Maybe it was all the romance books I read.

"Just good?" Meredith teased.

"It's fine. I mean, you guys know why we married—"

"Don't even try it. I've seen the looks he gives you," Destiny said, pursing her lips.

"Don't forget salt," I told her, watching as she added water and flour to her mixture.

"Right. Salt."

The women all checked their measurements and added salt to their dough.

"Have you heard from your ex?" Meredith asked, and I nodded.

"Andres is handling most of it, but we have a meeting with the lawyers soon," I said, dreading the confrontation.

Someone sent an anonymous print of the announcement for Gary's wedding to his ex-secretary to St. Elizabeth's, and it was forwarded to my new address.

I was surprised, but really, I felt nothing at all when I looked at the black-and-white image of him and his new wife.

Well, almost nothing. I felt pity for the woman, and I could only hope she didn't suffer what he'd put me through.

"Oh wow, you must be nervous," Sofia said, biting her bottom lip.

"A little bit," I lied.

I was a lot nervous.

"We're here for you, you know," Meredith said, bumping my shoulder, and I nodded.

"I know you are. Thanks."

It was true. These women had been there for me since day one. I didn't really have experience with girlfriends, but I valued them.

"I mean that. I appreciate you all. You've been so wonderful to me and Sammy. And I mean, of course, I'm including Andres with that. He's done so much for us, and I really have no idea why, or how to repay him," I said, knowing I was rambling.

"Uh, I have some ideas on how you can repay him, and they all involve a little *bowchickawowow*, and maybe spending a little time on your knees," Destiny said, raising her hand and swinging her hips in time with her bad singing.

The other ladies snorted and giggled and me, well, I blushed.

"Oh, I see you need no help in that department. Right on, girlfriend," she added with a nod.

"Can I tell you guys something? Or rather, can I ask you something personal?"

"You want tips on giving your husband a killer blow job? Cause I got tips," Destiny said.

"You only suck on the tip? I thought you were a deep throat kinda gal," Sofia replied.

"Oh my God, shut up," Destiny said, and I snorted.

"NO. I don't need tips. Well, not yet. Anyway, I mean, I don't know," I mumbled, knowing if I didn't say it fast, I ever would.

"Oh my God, spit it out," Destiny said.

"You don't swallow?" again from Sofia.

We were all giggling after that.

"Shut up, you guys," Meredith said, rolling her eyes in exasperation before facing me. "Come on, you can trust us. What is it, Ellie?" she asked.

"It's, um, well, when we go to bed at night, Andres is like the perfect gentleman—"

"Wait, you mean you guys haven't had sex?" Sofia asked, mouth gaping.

"What? No! I mean, yes, we have sex. Every night.

But it's me who starts it," I confessed, and my cheeks were burning with embarrassment.

"What do you mean? Like, is he not into it?" Meredith asked carefully.

"No, I mean, he seems very into it once we get going, but like, I'm the one who initiates it. He doesn't touch me unless I make the first move, and I wondered, does that mean there's something wrong? Like, with me, or shit, I don't know. I sound pathetic," I murmured, closing my eyes.

"Hold on. First, stop that," Sofia ordered in her best mom voice, and my eyes flicked to her. "There is nothing wrong with you. Nothing at all. And fuck whoever made you feel like that. Second, if *little Andres* is waking up for playtime, then it doesn't matter who touches who first. Clearly, the man wants you, too."

"*Little Andres?* Somehow, I doubt that," Destiny said, and everyone started chuckling again.

"True. I mean the guys are all big, bulky men and I know Adrik is definitely not little. So, how big we talking?" Sofia asked, waggling her eyebrows.

"You are such a horn dog, Sof," Destiny teased.

"I am not. It's research for the current book I'm writing," she replied with faux haughtiness.

I snorted.

"Okay. First, there is nothing little about *little Andres*," I admitted.

"Eeek! I knew it!" Sofia shouted.

The way she said it made me giggle like an idiot.

"Well, now that we solved that mystery, Ellie, let me tell you that man wants you. I mean, Marat said Andres has been more than a little distracted at work for weeks now. Also, ever since you moved in, your husband leaves work promptly at six every night," she announced.

"Why is that strange? Six is the usual time to leave work, isn't it?" I asked.

All three women shook their heads and rolled their eyes like I was the class dunce or something.

"Girl, do you not know a thing about your husband? He used to stay till ten every night. Serious overachiever. Adrik used to wonder if he was trying to take over the company."

"True, Marat said the same thing. But now that they know they're cousins—"

"Wait. What?" I asked, interrupting.

"Andres. His birth father was Adrik and Marat's father's brother. He told them the day of the wedding. Sorry, I thought you knew," Destiny said, frowning.

"Oh, right. Um, yeah. Excuse me. I'm just going to

check on Sammy," I muttered, wiping my hands free of dough on the dish towel I had sitting on my shoulder.

I was embarrassed.

I'd gotten caught not knowing something about Andres that he seemingly told a shitload of people on our wedding day.

But not me. Not his wife.

It would have been fine if he'd agreed to a fake relationship.

One just for show.

But he was the one who said he wanted this to be real. He was the one who practically demanded it.

But could a marriage be real if the couple never talked?

I didn't think it was possible for me to ever want to open up to anyone. But Andres was slowly burrowing past my walls and shields with his steady hands, his sweet attention, his unending patience, and his constancy.

But it wasn't enough. Suddenly, I wanted more from him. And the thought terrified me.

"Hey, whatcha building?" I asked Sammy as I stepped into the playroom where he was building a tower out of soft foam blocks around a giggling Michaela.

The room was cheerful, painted in bright colors with an entire wall of books and toys. There were bean bags and soft plush sofas and chairs.

A cushiony rug depicting gigantic cartoon cats sat in the center of the room.

It was lined with stuffed animals in every color and size, and a pile of foam blocks the children were busy playing with.

"Hello, Mommy. I'm making a tower," Sammy replied, and nodded sagely at his creation.

"Very nice," I told him, then turned my head to the nanny. "Has he been behaving?"

"Of course, Sammy is the best boy. Would you mind, ma'am? I must use the restroom," Nanny Rosa said.

I nodded my head at the older woman, and she rushed inside the connected restroom. Lucy was content in her bouncy chair, and Michaela and Sammy were getting along just fine.

This place was incredible. Every time I visited one of their homes, I was stunned by the warmth and charm I found within their walls.

Sofia and Adrik had been together the longest, but the man himself was rather intimidating. I hardly spoke to him, but I knew he loved his wife and daughter. Marat was just as crazy about Destiny and their baby, Lucy. But I couldn't say I spoke to the almost-too-handsome man more than a polite greeting when I saw him.

Josef was perhaps the friendliest to me, but that might be because I was friendliest with his wife. Meredith, of course, knew me better than the others. She'd seen me at my worst. When I'd been black and blue and torn up on the inside.

Gary's violent outbursts were never warranted. I knew that. I knew I never deserved them. Why I'd stayed as long as I did was anyone's guess.

It was something my therapist and I had talked about for hours on end.

The last time he hit me, I got away. And that was all that mattered.

The second Gary had tried to direct his violence towards Sammy, I left.

I needed to acknowledge what I did, what I accomplished, and through months of therapy, I finally learned to accept my decisions and to be content with the knowledge I'd gotten my son away from that mess.

It was still a work in progress.

I was still a work in progress.

Just like most people.

But I would never knowingly endanger my child.

Yes, I was nervous about Tuesday's meeting with my ex's lawyers.

But Andres said he had it handled, and I believed him.

What was currently occupying all the available space in my brain was something I shouldn't even care about.

We aren't a love match.

Maybe if I kept repeating that, it wouldn't bother me that Andres was keeping secrets.

Why wouldn't he tell me about Adrik and Marat? That they were his cousins?

I didn't know. But I was going to ask.

Old me, cowed me, would never have questioned my husband.

Hell.

I never cared one way or another about what Gary did. The man was more dictator than husband.

But I cared with Andres.

I didn't want to be kept in the dark or lied to. Even if only by omission.

Fuck that.

I wasn't old Ellie anymore.

No more boring pastels and pleasant expressions. No more "sure, whatever you like" to what someone asked of me.

I was learning to be strong again. To trust myself. And if that meant confronting my new husband with this, then I would.

Andres wasn't Gary.

He wouldn't hurt me.

I knew that as surely as I knew the sky was blue.

I trusted him.

I just had to talk to him, and everything would be okay.

I hope.

I knew the second I walked into the condo something was wrong.

There was a certain tension in the air. An energy I wasn't used to feeling, and I had to admit I was curious.

I knew nothing bad had happened from the reports I'd gotten from the driver and bodyguard I hired from Sigma International, Josef's security firm, to protect my wife and son when I wasn't there.

I knew I should probably ask Ellie if it was okay to call him that. My son. But since I was going to do it anyway, it was really a moot point.

Sammy greeted me with his usual enthusiastic squeal, followed by tackling my knees. He must have been snacking on something because his hands were liberally covered with a cheesy film, but I didn't mind. Clothes could be cleaned.

"Careful! Sorry, his hands are dirty. He was having a snack," Ellie said, and was about to rush over to take him from me, but I shook my head.

"It's fine," I said gently, stopping her in her tracks.

I lifted my boy up and gave him a spin, loving the sound of his giggles.

"How's my little man doing today?" I asked, knowing I was going to have a confrontation with his mother.

I shouldn't have gotten excited about that, but I did. Ellie in a mood was something to behold.

"Yayyy! I saw Mmm'cheala, and when we got home, Rocky was sleeping on my bed," he told me, the excitement of the day making his hazel eyes sparkle just like his mother's.

"Lucky kitty. So, you saw Michaela? Did you have fun?" I asked.

"Yeah, we played," he said, still grinning.

"What did you play?"

I listened to his enthusiastic tale that ended with Adrik's daughter knocking down his block tower, but then Nanny Rosa made them grilled cheeses with apple slices on the side and that fixed everything.

"So one grilled cheese and you two were pals again?" I asked, watching him nod with my eyebrows raised.

"Yup, Mommy says grilled cheeses are magic."

"That they are. Sammy, can you go wash up for dinner?" Ellie asked, smiling at her son.

"Yup, Mommy. I'm hungry!"

"You just had a snack," she chided, but I could see the love shining in her eyes as she spoke to him.

I wanted her to look at me like that. Well, maybe not exactly like that, but with feeling.

Soon.

I just had to be patient.

"Sammy, make sure you say your ABCs at least once before rinsing off the soap," she instructed.

She looked so cute, hands on her hips, using that unmistakable mom voice. So stern. So hot. It made me wonder if maybe she'd consider giving me instructions in the bedroom.

Goddamn.

She was so beautiful.

Today she was wearing a pair of stretchy jeans that hugged her perfect ass, and drew my eyes like a moth to a flame.

She wore a plain t-shirt on top and a small apron tied around her waist. Her hair looked a little wild, even though she attempted to hold it back from her face with some kind of stretchy headband.

I liked it wild. When we first met, Ellie's hair was short, like a pixie. Now it hovered just above her shoulders in choppy layers that made her big curls look even more tempting, resting just against the soft skin of her neck.

Fuck.

I wanted her so much. That pull I felt to her increased more and more each day.

She was so good. So pure.

I looked at the apron again, noting the different colors where she might have wiped her hands or spilled something, and grinned.

She was a fantastic cook. The entire condo smelled delicious from her efforts.

The telltale signs of a home-cooked meal were familiar now. Something I never expected. I grinned again, wondering what amazing thing she put together for us tonight.

Ellie was a wonder in the kitchen, but I never made demands of her. She didn't have to cook or clean or whatever. Hell, she could do anything she wanted.

I told her we could hire someone, or multiple

someones, to do chores and things like cooking. But she refused the offer and seemed to enjoy doing it.

So, I simply left her to it, giving her access to all the grocery delivery apps I had standing orders with so she could add whatever she liked to it.

I enjoyed eating whatever she made, so really it was a win-win. Ellie could cook all she wanted.

One thing I wouldn't budge on was the cleaning service.

She worked hard enough already just raising Sammy. I didn't need her to mop floors or wash toilets.

There was nothing demeaning in that sort of work, but we could afford the staff, and I insisted she use it.

"Hi," I said, pressing my lips together.

It was so damn hard not to go to her every time she entered a room. My heart pounded, my pulse raced.

All I wanted to do was gather her in my arms and smash my mouth to hers, to breathe in her air and taste her lips.

She always tasted so good. Like the lemon drop candies she kept in her purse.

"Hi," she replied, and I was struck again by the fact that something was wrong.

It was like a sixth sense where she was concerned. No. I wasn't psychic. I wasn't crazy enough to think that was even possible.

But I knew Ellie. I'd studied her.

Okay, maybe stalked was a better word, but I shrugged off the negativity associated with that.

I was crazy about the woman, so yeah, I knew her expressions.

Not all of them. But enough that I sensed she was upset about something.

I furrowed my brows and followed her as she turned her back on me and retreated to the kitchen.

Fuck.

The smells were even better in there.

Hints of garlic, basil, red wine, and tomatoes danced in the air. The unmistakable scent of fresh baked bread, and fuck, was that chocolate?

Did she make dessert, too?

I groaned and licked my lips. I'd taken to working out during my lunch hour just to keep fit. But it was worth it for a chance to have Ellie's cookies in my mouth.

Goddamn.

That thought sent my mind straight to the gutter.

"So when were you going to tell me Adrik and

Marat are your cousins?" she asked, shoulders stiff as she stirred something inside a pot.

"Huh?" I asked, thoroughly distracted by the tiny bow hovering right above her ass.

Like her ass was a present just for me. The little string dangling from the bow was practically begging me to tug it. To unwrap my wife like a fucking gift.

But I didn't.

I wouldn't.

I never touched my wife unless she moved first.

It was the only concession I made to her sensibilities.

I didn't know the details of her former marriage, but I knew her ex was already living on borrowed time.

Gary Peters was a walking dead man for the things he did. I just needed time before I could make that happen.

Right now there was too much attention on him to make his death not look like the cold-blooded fucking murder it would be.

I didn't need that kind of heat.

But wait, what did she just say?

"Who told you that?" I asked, curious.

"I was at Sofia's today. The wives talk."

Ellie shrugged, her back towards me, and I took a step closer to her. I had to bridge the distance, even if just an inch at a time. I couldn't help it.

It was always that way.

Whenever I was anywhere near her, it was always too far away. Feet, inches, whatever. The space between us was always too much.

Being close just wasn't good enough.

This pull, I felt, was like a compulsion.

No, it was so much more than that. It was like a gravitational force.

Ellie was my sun, or maybe I was her moon.

At any rate, I orbited her. Helpless to withstand the pull. Every fiber of my being attuned to her.

I didn't like her upset. But I was curious about it.

"I need you to tell me what's going on, Lupina," I said, watching in awe as she straightened her spine before facing me.

"Tell you what's going on? Sure. I'll do that when you tell me what else you're keeping from me," she said, hands on her hips.

"What do you mean?"

"Your messages are on the side table," she said, spinning back around to check the heat on the stove.

I frowned and walked to the little table where I tossed my keys. I hadn't noticed the little pad of pink

Post-It notes sitting there. I grabbed it and read the neatly scrawled handwriting.

Gabby called.

Twice.

I smirked. Gabby was my mother's oldest and dearest friend, and she was undoubtedly calling about my mother's upcoming birthday.

It was her sixtieth. A big deal, to say the least, and I was planning a party for her.

Something I should probably have told my wife, but really, I just hadn't thought of it.

"This makes you mad, Wife?" I asked, cocking my head as I watched my wife studiously ignoring me.

"Should it?" she snapped.

Hope began to build inside.

Was it possible I was winning her over? Did my bride of convenience care more than she let on?

All the while I felt like Ellie was the puppeteer and I her willing marionette. But maybe she felt like that, too.

Maybe she thought I was manipulating her, keeping secrets.

Hell, the woman didn't even have to pull on my strings to get me to come to her. I was so fucking gone for her.

Didn't she know how desperate I was for her? Couldn't she tell?

I would run miles.

Walk through fire.

Crawl over broken glass.

Complete any number of feats just for the chance to earn a smile from her lips.

"Thanks for taking the message," I said, tugging off my suit jacket and draping it over one of the kitchen stools.

"Thanks? Did you say thanks?" she asked, and her annoyance suddenly turned into anger.

"Yeah, thanks," I said, not really sure what I said wrong.

"You're actually thanking me for taking a message from some woman named Gabby I never even heard you mention?"

"Uhhhh," I said like the rocket scientist I obviously wasn't.

"Ellie, I don't know what to say right now."

"Fine. Whatever," she grumbled, then slammed her spatula on the counter.

"Ellie—" I started to explain, but my wife was all worked up.

And fuck, was she cute.

"You know what? Not fine. Not whatever."

"Ookayyy," I began, raising my hands like a robbery victim. "Ellie, I am going to need some context here."

"You want context? I'll give you context. What else about your life do I have to find out from my friends? And, well, are you cheating on me?"

"What?!" I was stunned.

"Adrik and Marat are your cousins? Like actual cousins? Some woman named Gabby keeps calling for you and apparently, she doesn't need to leave her number because you have it already. Just how many secrets are you keeping from me?"

My mouth was hanging open as I watched timid, sweet little Ellie tear me a new asshole.

Cheating on her? Was she nuts?

Her eyes were sparkling with anger and annoyance, which was very encouraging, considering I wanted her to fall for me.

But the flash of hurt I saw, even though it lasted a mere second, was too much.

I never wanted to hurt her.

Not ever.

Clearly, we needed to talk.

I just didn't know if she was going to let me get a word in edgewise.

Stupid dumb lying liar.

Lies of omission were still lies.

I hated feeling like this.

Angry and uncertain. And just plain hurt.

Gary cheated on me, but I never cared. In fact, I was grateful when he had other women. It meant he'd leave me alone.

Not that he ever bothered me much for sex.

Sure, my ego had taken a beating, but I simply assumed it was due to our age difference or preferences in the bedroom. Whatever it was, I never missed sex with Gary.

But I would with Andres.

Goddamn him. Please don't lie to me.

Andres promised we wouldn't have that. He said

no lies, no cheating. But this sure felt like a breach of promise to me.

Strange women calling my house to speak with my husband twice in a matter of hours?

Yeah. That was a big fucking no-no, too.

Andres stood there, looking deliciously rumpled from his day at work, and I wanted to dump the bowl of salad I'd just put together right over his big, dumb head.

He'd removed his jacket, loosened his tie, and the top four buttons on his shirt were undone, giving me a tantalizing view of the chest hair I loved to nuzzle.

Sonofabitch.

Why did he have to look so good?

I, on the other hand, looked exactly like I'd spent the last three hours traveling back to Manhattan from Long Island, wrangling Sammy into a bath, ordering then putting away a grocery delivery, and getting everything ready for a fresh pasta dinner with a cherry chocolate cake for dessert.

Not that he'd be getting any of my chocolate cherries for the foreseeable future.

"Ellie, I am going to need some context here," his deep voice rumbled, and I snapped my attention back to him.

"You want context? I'll give you context. What else about your life do I have to find out from my friends? And, well, are you cheating on me?"

"What?!"

"Adrik and Marat are your cousins? Like actual cousins? Some woman named Gabby keeps calling for you and apparently, she doesn't need to leave her number because you have it already. Just how many secrets are you keeping from me?"

I said, inhaling roughly. I was on a roll now, and I couldn't stop. even if it meant making an ass out of myself.

"Today I was with my friends, and they knew more about you than I did. Do you know how I felt? Can you even imagine? Anything else about your life I need to find out from my friends?"

Anger and jealousy were not emotions I enjoyed feeling, but suddenly I was overwhelmed by them. Thank goodness Sammy was preoccupied at the moment.

We'd never had a fight or argument in front of my son, and I really didn't want to. Not about this.

"What are you talking about?" Andres asked, looking truly baffled.

Men were so dense sometimes.

I shook my head and tried for a calm I did not feel when I finally addressed him again.

"Adrik and Marat are your cousins? Like actual cousins? Some woman named Gabby keeps calling for you and apparently, she doesn't need to leave her number because you have it already. Just how many secrets are you keeping from me?"

"Ellie, I'm so sorry," he said, and I was stunned.

He was apologizing. To me. In my experience, men didn't do that. But Andres wasn't like anyone else I'd ever met. He was constantly surprising me.

I just didn't know what that meant.

"Why are you apologizing? Is Gabby your girl-friend?" I asked, hating that my voice cracked.

Having a woman call for my husband twice in the last hour after I'd been feeling a little bad about him not telling me about his cousin status to his bosses, well, it just pushed me over the edge.

Things with Andres had been going well.

Or, at least, I thought they were going well. But maybe I was fooling myself. Maybe this was all a mistake.

"What? No! Gabby is not my girlfriend. I am not cheating on you. I would never cheat on you. Ellie, you are *my wife*," he growled, sounding angry.

"I know. I was there when we got married," I

shouted, feeling horrible now for getting mad, and a little embarrassed.

"Ellie—"

"No, just let me finish. Look, I know you are doing everything you promised to help me not lose custody of Sammy to Gary, but I don't really know anything about you," I said, hating how weak I sounded.

"That's not true. Don't say that. Don't ever say that," Andres said, and goddamn myself for wanting to believe him.

"Ellie, Gabby is my mother's best friend."

"Your mother?"

"Yeah. Mom's birthday is coming up next month, and Gabby asked to be in charge of the party. It's her sixtieth," he told me, and I stood there gaping like a moron.

How could I be so wrong?

I felt like a total piece of shit for being jealous of his mother's best friend.

"Shit. I'm sorry," I said, shaking my head.

"It's not your fault. I should have told you. I didn't mean to keep it a secret, it just slipped my mind," he said, reaching for my hand.

I let him take it, needing the connection to ground me.

Shit. When did that happen? When did I start needing him?

"Come here," he whispered, pulling me into an embrace, and I allowed it.

I pressed my forehead against his chest and stood there, letting him hold me in the kitchen while dinner simmered on the stove.

Like we were just a normal couple, making up after a misunderstanding.

I wish that was true.

*H*oly fuck.

Was Ellie jealous?

They said hope springs eternal.

As I listened to my wife and took in her anger and her beautiful jealousy, a tiny seed of hope took root deep inside my soul.

It was sick.

I was an asshole.

But the idea that she might be even a tiny bit possessive of me had my dick hard and my heart hammering inside my chest.

Maybe my beauty would learn to love her beast.

Maybe even sooner than I hoped.

Let me in, Lupina.

Love me like I love you.

Please.

I wrapped my arms around her tighter, breathing in her fresh scent and trying to control my baser instincts to lay claim to her right there.

I wanted her naked and panting, writhing beneath me. I wanted to fill her with my cock. Stuff her so full she didn't know where she ended, and I began.

I wanted to make her come so hard she forgot her own name.

I wanted, fuck yes, I wanted.

Later, I told myself. After dinner, and after we put Sammy to bed.

I would do all that and more.

Later.

"Come here."

That was all he had to say to get me to relinquish the stranglehold I had on my anger. What was left felt worse.

Like a horrible combination of confusion, desperation, disbelief, embarrassment, and hope.

I kept telling myself I'd proposed to Andres out of desperation.

Not because I liked him.

Or wanted him.

Or felt an off the charts powerful attraction to him.

Being a realist, I knew I needed help, and I knew he had connections.

He was just the sort of weapon a girl like me needed in her arsenal.

Someone lethal, ambitious, and determined, who oozed masculine prowess and protective vibes.

I knew a little bit about Andres. Like the fact he didn't come from money. He earned his fortune through his own brilliance and hard work.

I admired that. Respected him for it. Just like I admired how readily he'd taken to my son.

Those protective vibes I was talking about before were amplified a zillion times when it came to Sammy. Just the idea of Andres as a dad, even a stepdad, was enough to make my ovaries go off like fireworks.

Oh my.

It might sound crazy, but in those few minutes when he held me inside of the commercial-grade kitchen, it was like time stopped.

Like the connection between actual time and my brain had short-circuited.

The man was dangerous.

Andres was like no one I'd ever met. When I said I was sheltered growing up, I meant it.

And as he held me, a typhoon of memories came flooding into my befuddled brain.

Maybe it was his big, powerful body wrapped

around mine that did it. Or that crazy sexy scent that seemed to cling to his bronzed skin.

I didn't know. I didn't care. I just held on and tried to keep up while my mind raced.

Andres was so smart. Well-educated. A genius at the company, I'd heard the wives and even their husbands praise him.

Would he care that I rarely attended actual school? That I preferred reading smut to reading the Wall Street Journal?

Shit. I felt so damn inadequate sometimes, but Andres seemed to instinctively feel my self-doubt growing, and he hugged me tighter.

I closed my eyes and saw images of my Dad. He was so much older than me.

He was a gruff man. Rarely smiled. And he preferred I stayed home.

I had nannies and tutors, stuff like that. I did attend a private school for a bit. Got to experience high school, went to prom.

But I only went to college for a semester. Didn't even finish.

I went back and was just as happy to stay home as my father was to keep me there.

I didn't realize what it was doing to me. What I

was doing to myself. How it would hurt me in the end.

Inexperience and ignorance were the real enemies.

I was green as grass when I met Gary. I didn't know what he was or recognize the signs.

Maybe I was broken.

And this next part was hard to admit, but my therapist helped me get there, and Andres made me feel brave enough to face it. So, hate the past or not, I had to own mine.

I didn't know a damn thing about life when I married Gary. I traded the gilded cage my father built me for a crude one forged by a man who had no depth of feelings for anything other than himself.

Gary had some money, but most of it was loans. Stuff he owed. We used my trust fund to buy the condo where we lived after our wedding.

Where he still lived.

And I allowed it. I thought sure, I can pay, why not? We were married. It was okay. I hardly flinched when he insisted on things being a certain way.

Gary had a lot of quirks. Like how his laundry was to be put away and such, but thankfully, he wanted a service to do all that.

Still, I could have fought. Could have argued. But

I didn't. I just thought that was how things were in a marriage.

No, I did not blame myself for Gary's abuse. But I could have been more proactive about protecting myself.

And I could have started when I was younger and under my father's thumb.

The thing about it was I didn't realize I was being manipulated by the men in my life who should have been supporting me to become all I could be.

Of course, now I knew better. With therapy, I learned to let go of what I couldn't change, and to embrace my future. The future I chose.

With Andres and Sammy.

Leaving my horrible marriage and the relative security of Gary's home was a rude, rough awakening for me. Moving into St. E's, while much appreciated, was a lot different from the places I'd lived.

They had an outstanding staff, and with Meredith taking over and Josef's company providing security, well, it was safer and better than ever.

But those first few weeks had been difficult.

Wrapping my head around the fact that I'd been hurt by the man who swore to love and honor me was stunning.

It was unbelievable.

I didn't mourn Gary or my marriage. On the contrary, I rejoiced at my newfound freedom, and that was maybe the thing that made me feel the guiltiest.

I should have left long before he raised his hands.

I didn't love him.

I didn't want him.

I didn't even like him.

So what the hell was I doing with him?

I guess I thought it was expected of me. He was the father of my child, and I'd made a vow, right?

But sometimes life wasn't so cut and dry.

Sometimes it was messy and complicated.

Gary was a douchebag—admitting that part was easy.

He deserved to rot for what he did. And I knew I wasn't to blame. Nothing I'd ever done in my whole life warranted him putting hands on me.

As for what he'd tried to do to my son? What he was still trying to do?

Get visitation. Fight me for custody.

Those were things I would never allow to happen.

Over my dead body.

"You okay?" Andres asked, and I nodded, still too raw to speak.

I guessed he accepted my response because he said nothing else. Just hugged me and rubbed my back while inside my brain I spiraled.

Gary had never shown an interest in Sammy. He spent no time whatsoever with my sweet boy.

He hardly even acknowledged him. I was sure Gary was just using this as an excuse. A pitiful attempt to hurt me.

This was just him throwing a temper tantrum because his plans to get my father's company backfired.

Gary was a fucking pig, and he deserved to drop dead.

Maybe that made me a bad person, but I was fine with it.

I was worried, yes, but I trusted Andres to find a solution.

That sonofabitch Gary only wanted to use Sammy as a pawn, I was sure of it.

But I didn't really understand how it all tied together with my father's company.

I mean, I knew I inherited the lion's share, but I also knew there were stipulations that would force a sale.

My father didn't ever want me running Maxwell Mining.

I knew that better than I knew my name.

Maybe that should have made me angry.

Maybe the feminist in me should have fought with my father.

I could have maybe convinced him that women could and did run companies bigger than Maxwell Mining.

Maybe.

But the truth, *the real truth*, was I didn't care about the company.

I had no desire to learn about the family business or to run Maxwell Mining.

None at all.

I didn't know if that made me a traitor to my sex or not.

My interests leaned towards things like cooking, baking, raising my son, reading, even crocheting. I mean I liked other stuff, too.

I just didn't like business.

And yes, I realized what a privileged life I'd led.

My father's tendencies towards misogyny just enabled me.

I mean, maybe it was a lazy point of view to want the lifestyle I wanted, but I couldn't help it.

And really, didn't it make me the ultimate feminist to want the life I wanted? Even if it didn't include running a multimillion dollar company?

Even now that I had a few more years under my belt, one divorce, a new husband, and a son to raise, I was still fundamentally the same.

Those things hadn't made me want to join the corporate world.

I would have sold Maxwell Mining to the first person who offered after my father died, but Gary had challenged the will right off the bat.

Even though my father's lawyer was supposed to handle that sale, it was the fact I was inheriting the proceeds that Gary took issue with.

Like he somehow deserved my inheritance.

Poor Gar. He had honestly thought marrying me would grant him the position he'd always coveted. But that wasn't my father's way.

Dad didn't think a woman could run the company, true. But he also wasn't a fan of nepotism.

My father's will had been written to ensure my ex-husband would never get his hands on the company. Dad and I had a strained relationship, but he never liked Gary.

Now I knew why. I only wished he'd been the kind of dad who would have told me how he felt.

But he wasn't, and he didn't. And I couldn't change the past.

I wouldn't want to.

The past brought me Sammy.

And my son was worth everything I'd been through.

That wasn't the issue. What really had me wringing my hands day in and day out was my current marriage.

I'd ignored the fact that I was actually a lot more attracted to Andres on a personal level than I'd ever intended to be.

But I really should have known better than to allow myself to get caught up in feelings for Andres.

I mean, this marriage was one I'd proposed, born of need and convenience.

What kind of idiot was I to allow myself even the fantasy that he might care for me someday?

Like really care for me.

I closed my eyes and focused on my breathing, taking note of the aromas in the air, I could tell dinner needed more time to simmer.

Just enough time for us to hash this out, because we needed to do that. I needed to do that.

I had to clear the air, otherwise I might combust.

Holy shit.

I think I maybe caught feelings for my husband.

And that was the dumbest thing I could have done.

CHAPTER TWENTY ELLIE

Andres already did everything I'd asked of him.

More than I'd hoped for.

Even if I didn't really understand his motives for marrying me.

It didn't matter, because he still did it.

I had no right to ask for more.

My emotions were wild like a rollercoaster as he wrapped me in his spicy cologne scented embrace.

Andres nuzzled my neck, and I felt his beard tickling the skin there as he pressed his lips to me.

Holy damp panties.

I didn't know what this was. Wasn't sure how to label our relationship. But it sure felt like more than a marriage of convenience.

And no, I didn't want to think about my jealous display or why I'd even felt murderous rage when that woman had called asking for Andres.

Of course, now that I knew she was his mother's best friend, I felt a little sheepish about my reaction.

Apparently, I was a little possessive of my husband.

Those feelings were unexpected, and I didn't know what to do with it.

I also did not want to think about why I'd gotten so sad when Sof, Des, and Mer all seemed to know my husband had recently let it be known to everyone—*except me*—that Adrik and Marat were his cousins.

Maybe it was all that trust I'd placed in Andres' hands that had me reacting this way. Or maybe it was because every single night since we'd gotten married, no matter how many times I said I wouldn't cave, I found myself incapable of ignoring his presence.

I ached for that man.

In my most secret places, I needed him.

Wanted him.

I'd never felt that way about anyone, and it was disarming. I felt completely undone. Left naked and raw and open to ridicule.

If I'd known that would happen, I would never have proposed to him.

Andres didn't love me.

He never claimed to, and he sure as fuck didn't owe me anything.

But I was behaving like a jealous spouse.

And I couldn't have that.

I shouldn't have that.

Fuck. Damn.

I was seriously losing my shit.

I was falling for my husband, and I didn't know how to stop.

"Ellie."

Andres pulled back from our embrace, his stormy gaze freezing me in place.

Awareness surged, and that attraction I felt simmering at all times increased until it felt like a bonfire.

Ripples of need coursed through my bloodstream. Heat sizzled between us, and I felt a pull so strong I swayed on my feet.

Just like a magnet, I thought inanely.

His hands flexed on my waist, and I couldn't deny how he made me feel. I was drawn to him, incapable of resisting the pleasure that surged in my veins every time we touched.

Did I even want to try?

CHAPTER TWENTY-ONE ANDRES

If she only knew.

Ellie wanted to know how many secrets I was keeping, well, goddamn, I wasn't about to tell her.

What could I say?

Why, yes Ellie, I have been keeping things from you.

Like the fact I'm obsessed with you. Completely and totally fucking unhinged when it comes to you.

I spend every waking moment thinking about you, wanting you, needing you.

I'm like a fucking junky with an addiction I have no control over. But it isn't smack that has me off the rails, it's you.

I am fucking addicted to you and your smiles, your

kisses, the way you sigh in your sleep, the face you make when you come.

Fuck.

Fuck.

FUCK.

I had so many fucking secrets. But I couldn't tell her any of them.

"Ellie," I said her name again, stepping back from her tempting warmth.

I couldn't touch her and keep my train of thought. I was only human, for fuck's sake.

"I'm sorry if I kept things from you. It was unintentional. I wasn't trying to hold anything back," I said, carefully weighing my words.

I wanted to explain. To tell her how much she meant to me without sending her running. But like always, I was overthinking it.

"Andres," she sighed. "I'm sorry, I just don't want to do this. I-I can't, I won't—"

Ellie dropped her chin and shook her head. Turning around, she gave me her back.

My heart was pounding so hard, squeezing tightly inside my chest until I couldn't breathe.

Panic gripped me.

She won't? She can't? What did she mean she didn't want to do this?

"No. No! Don't tell me you don't want to do this, Lupina," I said, sputtering my words.

Fear made me choke.

Suddenly, I was so fucking scared.

Was she trying to leave me already?

The possibility made me sick to my stomach.

She can't leave me. I won't let her.

I'd do anything to keep her. Promise anything. Give anything. Even trick her.

If I had to fuck her into submission right there on the countertop to get her to agree to stay, I would.

"I fucked up by not telling you everything, but there's no going back for us, Ellie. I won't let you leave," I growled, placing my hand on her elbow.

I wanted to force her to face me, but I needed to calm down first.

"What? No, I didn't mean that. I just meant, I can't have you shutting me out. I don't want to feel like this," she said, her voice low.

"Like what?" I asked, right behind her now.

I needed to see her face when she was speaking so I could gauge how she felt.

Ellie heaved a sigh, but she turned around. Her eyes were still downcast, and I couldn't help it then.

I reached out and touched my finger to her chin, lifting gently until she looked at me.

"We're married now. We do this together. Please, just talk to me. Explain to me what I did wrong and how I can make it up to you, Wife."

Curiosity burned inside me like a living thing as I watched her processing my request.

Would she indulge me? Or tell me to fuck off?

I was eager to know. Anxious for her decision on how to handle me.

My Lupina was no mouse, no matter what she thought or how others viewed her.

I knew it, but that wasn't enough. I needed her to know it, too.

"I'm sorry I—" Ellie started.

Her expression was so forlorn, it pained me to witness it. That I had caused her even a second's displeasure made me ridiculously angry with myself.

She deserved better. For her, I would do better.

"Don't apologize. Just tell me what's on your mind," I said, interrupting her.

"Okay, fine," she muttered and heaved a sigh.

I bit back my smirk.

She was so fucking cute when she got annoyed.

Her gold-green eyes flashed with temper, and

fuck, my cock was already half-hard just looking at her.

"Andres, I just need you to promise to talk to me, okay? No matter what. Telling your bosses they're your cousins was probably emotional for you, and I'd like to be there for you when you have something like that going on. I'm your wife," she murmured.

Pleasure filled me at her quiet declaration, but I held my tongue. My wife clearly had more to say.

"Even if it's hard or ugly. I want to know. Maybe I can help," she added. "I just don't want to feel like I did something wrong when you go all quiet. If I did something to make you upset or something, I need you to tell me so we can discuss it like adults."

"You think I'm angry with you?" I asked, truly stunned.

"I don't know if you're angry with me or if you're anything with me because you don't tell me. I don't like not knowing. When I was married to Gary, he always played these little games, and he just made me feel bad all the time."

"I make you feel bad?" I asked, my eyes even wider.

"No! No," she said, shaking her head, and some of my tension eased.

I rubbed my hand over my face, trying for a calm I didn't feel.

"Ellie, what are you really saying? I need you to tell me more, please," I said.

It was only through years of working a high-pressure job that I wasn't a bumbling mess right then. I wanted to drop to my knees and beg forgiveness for something I didn't even know what.

This woman had me by the balls, and she didn't even know it.

"Maybe I shouldn't have said anything," she whispered.

"No. Don't do that. You can talk to me, Ellie. No Lies. Just truth. Always," I told her, meaning every word.

The last thing I ever wanted to do was ignore this. I didn't want her upset, but we needed to hash this out. Whatever this was.

Fuck.

I'd spent months mooning over this woman. Testing the strength of my resolve. Battling my attraction by holding back and staying away.

Every second apart from her was sheer fucking torture. I was head over fucking heels. But I knew she wasn't there.

Not yet.

I need her to be.

I want her to be.

But how was I supposed to make a woman like her fall in love with a guy like me?

I thought I had a pretty good plan. And it had been working so far. Every night my wife crawled into bed beside me, and every night the tension between us tightened until she came to me.

Sometimes it started with the brush of her leg against mine, or Ellie would drape her arm over my side. She'd touch me first, then I'd turn and pull her into my embrace.

I was always ready, willing, and waiting. Helpless to deny my feelings for her and the need to bury my length inside her warm, wet, willing body.

The sex we shared was phenomenal.

Fantastic.

At least, I thought it was.

But if I made her feel bad, I'd have to kick my own fucking ass.

I frowned.

Hard.

She always got off when we fucked. I made sure of it. Sometimes multiple times.

But had I grossly misjudged the physical aspects

of our relationship? Was I somehow not leaving my wife satisfied?

The mere thought that I was a selfish prick in that way made me want to fucking rage.

I was going to find out exactly what I was doing wrong the second we went to bed that night. And I was going to make sure I never did it again.

My Lupina never had a thing to fear from me. I would always take care of her.

Now I just had to prove it.

Turning my attention back to my wife who was still talking, I ran my hand back over my face and tuned back in to her words.

"This is so embarrassing," she said.

I guided her to one of the kitchen stools and held it out as she climbed into the seat, taking the one beside her.

"No secrets. No lies, remember? Talk to me."

I would keep repeating it until she believed me.

"Okay, maybe if I explain from the beginning. See, when I was a kid, I was always on the outside. My father loved me, but he was a busy man. An important man. I was raised by nannies," she started.

"Where was your mother?" I asked.

Yeah, I'd read the background report on Ellie Maxwell that I'd received from Josef's team back when Ellie first met his wife, Meredith. The man was overprotective to a fault, but I couldn't blame him.

Read the report? Ha.

I had the fucking thing memorized.

"My mother died when I was too young to remember, and Dad never remarried. When Gary walked into my life, I was just the right amount of lonely and desperate for attention, I ate it up."

"Don't talk about yourself like that, Ellie. You're not responsible for his behavior," I started, but she shook her head.

"I know that. But I am responsible for mine. And I. Ate. It. Up," she said, and I could see the self-loathing on her face.

It made my blood boil. To think she blamed herself at all for that vile prick's behavior.

That was just another strike against the asshole. Just another thing he stole from my wife along with her inner peace.

And I was going to take it back from him. I was going to reclaim my Lupina's pride, her peace, her dignity from him. And I was going to do it in flesh and blood.

"At first, I thought Gary was gentle and sweet. He was complimentary, and never demanding. I married him the second he asked, so damn hungry to feel a connection with just one person," she said, her voice cracking with emotion.

"It didn't matter that he wasn't overly romantic with me. I mean, I didn't know any better. And when he made excuses and stayed away most nights after we were married, I was more than okay with it. I assumed he was busy," she confessed, and I could tell by the set of her shoulders how humiliated she felt.

Anger on her behalf rose inside of me like the tide, but I swallowed it down. Gary was a piece of shit.

He'd tricked her. Used her. Made her feel unworthy of love and affection. And that was before the motherfucker laid hands on her.

Oh, I was counting down the fucking days until I could make him pay. All debts required payment, and his bill was just about fucking due.

"He wanted a child, and I wanted to be a mother. We needed some help, but after seeing a doctor, I got pregnant right away. That was good for both of us, really. Gary moved into a separate room because he said my tossing and turning kept him up at night. I didn't argue. It was better for me, too," she whispered, and I hated myself for asking, but I had to know.

"Did he hurt you? In the bedroom, I mean," I whispered, fighting against my fury.

"Oh, um, no, not like that. Not the way you mean," she said, and her cheeks turned red.

"Ellie," I murmured.

"Um, Gary wasn't m-my first," she whispered, not looking at me.

Surprise followed by jealousy followed by relief slammed into me. The last bit took me completely by surprise.

I exhaled slowly. The idea of her with anyone else made me want to commit fucking murder, but there was another part of me.

A selfless part I didn't even recognize since I so seldom saw it, that felt pure fucking joy that someone other than her piece of shit ex had had eased her into womanhood.

"I, um, *lost it* on prom weekend," she added.

I closed my eyes trying not to picture beautiful teenaged Ellie losing her cherry to some fucking high school punk.

But still, I had to admit the image was better than her ex.

"Okay. Good. Keep going," I growled.

"But I hadn't been with anyone else until my wedding night. I never knew why he wanted to wait, but I understood soon after when we were on our honeymoon. Gary had a hard time, um, rising to the occasion. He said it was my fault. My soft body wasn't appealing to him. And I was just always apologizing for it," she said.

"Ellie," I growled, but she shook her head.

"Just let me finish, okay? I have no misgivings about my body or how I look, and I am fine with it. This body gave me Sammy and I love it, I have to. Understand?"

I nodded. I couldn't do anything but nod. I needed her to keep talking.

"But Gary went quiet on me after the pregnancy, then he started with the games. He would tell me I was this burden, that I was this princess that he had to take care of and how sick I made him. He made me feel like I was nothing. Like I needed to apologize for my existence. I-I don't want to feel like that again. I can't apologize to you for being human and—"

"Ellie, no. Stop it," I grunted. "Listen to me. I don't know what I did to make you feel this way, but I am so fucking sorry."

"You don't have to apologize," she said, shaking her head, but the tears pricking her eyes made me feel so goddamn low.

"Yes. I clearly fucking do need to apologize, Lupina. You're my wife. I never want you to have feelings like that. I never want to make you feel how he made you feel. Not fucking ever."

"Andres, you don't have to say things like that to me," she said, shaking her head.

"Things like what?"

"Things that you would say to someone you actively pursued. Look, I know you only did this, married me, cause I asked you to. But why did you? I mean, really why did you marry me?"

"Don't you know?" I growled in frustration.

"Andres?"

"Okay, you've obviously had a rough day, and I contributed to that, I own that, and I am so fucking sorry," I growled, rubbing my hand over my face.

"Maybe on an intellectual level you knew Gary was a piece of shit, but inside you somewhere there is a piece of you that believes you deserved how he treated you, Ellie, and I won't have it. Not in this house. Not in this marriage."

"That's not-t true," she whispered, but I could see the wheels turning.

"Don't finish that lie. Think about it for a second. You bought into some of the horseshit that fucking vermin spouted. But I'm here now and I'm telling you no more."

Her eyes blinked slowly as she faced me, and I watched with quiet pride as she straightened her shoulders.

"You are not a puppy, Ellie Ramirez. You're not a mouse. You're not a doormat."

"What am I then?" she whispered the question.

"You are a fucking she-wolf. My Lupina. And I'm gonna keep telling you that until you believe it. Until you toss that gorgeous head back and howl like the motherfucking badass mama wolf I know you are. Hear me?"

"Yes, Andres," she said, eyes wide.

"Good. Now, you want to know why I married you? If I really want you? Gimme your hand," I growled, taking it before she could offer it and placing it over my rock hard length.

"Feel that? That's all for you, Angel."

"Andres," she whimpered, then swallowed.

Images of her throat working to suck down my length filled me, making my pants even tighter.

Fuck. Me.

"Any minute now Sammy could come running in here, otherwise I'd have you bent over with my cock buried in that hot pussy, showing you how much I want you. But I'll do that later," I murmured, letting go of her hand.

But she kept it right fucking there.

Right. Fucking. There. On my dick.

Her small palm stroked my cock over my suit pants, and if I wasn't used to practicing my iron fucking will whenever I was around her, I'd have come inside my boxers like some horny kid.

"Anytime I do something to make you doubt me, or yourself, you tell me right away, Wife. Promise me."

"I don't doubt you, Andres."

"Promise me," I repeated, groaning as she gripped me harder.

"Okay. Yes, I promise," she whispered.

"Good Girl," I grunted, pressing my mouth to hers and taking her hand off my dick.

I wanted to punch myself in the face for doing that, but I was seconds from blowing.

"We'll finish that later," I promised.

"O-okay. And I'm sorry, too. I was just, well, the girls were talking, and they know more about you than I do. And it made me feel bad. I mean, Adrik and Marat are your cousins and you told them at the wedding, but I wondered when you were going to tell me, and I felt bad," she said.

"I didn't mean to not tell you, and I feel like shit for making you feel bad," I told her, going for the truth.

Ellie shook her head, as if to stop me from apologizing. I wasn't about to tell her I loved her. Not yet. But I needed to give her something.

I cupped her cheeks in my hand and waited for her soft hazel eyes to meet mine.

"Try to understand, Wife, when I'm with you, it's all I can do to remember to breathe."

"What?" she asked, her gorgeous eyes blinking up at me.

"Mommy! When is dinner?" Sammy called, his little feet making slapping noises on the hardwood floor.

"In a few minutes, Sweetie," she called out, her gaze still locked on mine. "Andres, you don't have to say things like that," she said, her small hands touching my sides.

Fuck.

I loved having her hands on me.

"Yes, I do. Because it's the truth. Now, listen to me, Gary is a piece of shit. He never deserved you. But I do, Angel. I will always treat you right. And if I don't, just tell me, trust me, and I will turn it around. I fucking swear it."

"I know. And I trust you."

"Good. You also need to know you never have to apologize to me for anything."

"Andres, that's not—"

"Yes, it is. And fuck him for making you feel bad for existing. That piece of shit," I growled, having to close my eyes to control my temper.

Her mouth opened, and I knew she needed to hear this as much as I needed to say it.

"Listen to me, Ellie Ramirez, the fact that you're alive and you're human, that you're *you*, that's why I was fucking born. No, don't look away, look at me," I said, cupping one hand behind her neck.

"I-I," she stuttered, and I knew what she meant cause I fucking felt it, too.

She might not be ready for this.

I might be moving too fast.

But I need her to know.

"You're not responsible for his failures, or for mine. You never were, and you never will be. I made a vow to you, Ellie, my wife, and I will do better. I fucking promise. You believe me?"

"Andres, you don't have to do better," she said, shaking her head.

This woman.

This beautiful, warm, vibrant, powerful woman.

She holds the key to my heart in her small, capable hands, and she doesn't even know it.

This woman, my Ellie, is everything.

"Nonnegotiable. I'll do better. I'll be better because it's what you deserve," I said, my gaze unwavering as I stared into her gold-flecked irises.

"You've done so much. Everything you promised. You don't have to do anything else," she said, but I shook my head.

"I'm not even close to finished," I growled, dropping a hard kiss on her mouth.

"Mommy! I'm hungry! HUNGRYYYYY!" Sammy called again, and I pulled back just as he ran into the kitchen, roaring like a pint-sized monster.

My grin was real as I watched him close his mouth then slow down when he saw us. Careful to keep still, allowing him to see my arms around his mother in a gentle hug.

It was important he understood I would never hurt her. Sammy needed security and routine.

I'd been reading about childcare and how abusive situations could have lasting effects on a child's psyche.

It filled me with murderous rage when I thought

of any harm that prick Gary's actions could have on Sammy's precious little head.

Biting back on my thirst for revenge, I focused on what I could do to make it better.

No, I could not erase the past, but I could make sure he had a good future.

That we all had a good future.

And that started right here, with Ellie in my arms and *our son* running inside the kitchen, seeing us hugging, asking about dinner because he had no other cares in the world.

Sammy needed to know that love and affection could exist between two consenting adults. That his mother was in good hands, and so was he.

As our son, he would always know he was safe.

That boy is so safe with me. So is his mom.

"It's almost ready, Sweet Boy. How about we play a game until Mommy calls us?" I said, not taking my eyes off Ellie.

"Okay," Sammy agreed.

But he was still watching, so I leaned down to give his mother a small peck on the mouth. The shy smile she gave me in return was so worth it.

And when I picked up Sammy so he could kiss his mom, too, well, Ellie full on giggled.

Fucking adorable.

"You two cuties need to get out of my kitchen so I can concentrate, or we'll never eat," she teased, ruffling Sammy's hair.

"Cuties?" I said, frowning, unable to help myself.

"You know you're cute. Now shoo," Ellie said, rolling her eyes.

"Uh oh. We better get out of here, Sammy, so Mommy can finish cooking."

"Yeah! Let's get out of here, Dad!" Sammy giggled as I placed him back on the floor.

He ran inside the other room squealing, unaware of the effect his words had on me. My heart stuttered, and I faltered a step.

My gaze flashed back to Ellie's, and I saw her swallow. Her skin was white as loose leaf.

"Oh, um, Sammy heard Michaela talk about Adrik and she called him Daddy. Then he asked what he should call you. H-his father was never really a part of things, but he, Gary that is, insisted Sammy call him Papa. I thought maybe if it was okay with you, Sammy could call you Dad?" she asked, biting her lower lip.

I cleared my throat, inhaling a sharp breath.

Fuck. Was it hot in there?

I nodded my head like one of those stupid bobble

head dolls. Trying to force the moisture in my eyes to go back inside my head.

"Yeah. That's okay," I replied, ignoring the husky quality my voice took on.

Dad.

That little boy wanted to call me Dad.

Pride, the likes of which I never felt, filled me, and before I could do or say anything else, I crossed the couple of steps separating me from Ellie, and I pulled my wife to me with one hand on her neck.

Then I crushed her mouth beneath mine.

I didn't trust myself to touch her with any part of me other than on her lips and where my one hand gripped the back of her neck.

"Andres," she whimpered.

"Thank you. Thank you so fucking much," I told her.

"Come play, Dad!" Sammy called out from the other room.

"I better go see what my son wants to play," I whispered back.

Ellie nodded, and I had to admit, I may have strutted a bit as I walked inside the living room and play-tackled my sweet little boy.

My son. He's mine now, too.

Nothing could have prepared me for the wave of

emotions that had crashed into me when Sammy had called me Dad.

It was an honor. One I'd never expected.

Goddamn.

I loved that woman. I loved her boy.

They were part of me now. Ellie and Sammy were mine. I had them in my home and in my heart.

Mine on paper.

And in person.

I had a family.

A wife and son I adored.

I would do anything to keep them safe and secure. Anything to make them happy.

And I will never let them go.

CHAPTER TWENTY-THREE ELLIE

After dinner, I expected things to be a little awkward between us. But when I excused myself to the bathroom, Andres offered to read to Sammy and tuck him in.

I could tell he was enamored with the whole calling him *Dad* thing, and I had to admit, tears pricked my eyes every time my boy uttered the word.

Sammy looked so happy and proud, calling Andres Dad. And it felt so right.

Andres was kind, attentive, and patient with Sammy. Hell, he'd already spent more time with him than Gary ever had.

Sammy had nothing of his biological father in him. He looked like me. His dark hair and hazel eyes were so like mine. He was a wonderful little boy, and I was lucky to have him.

After kissing his head and asking him if he was okay with Dad reading his bedtime story, Sammy had practically pushed me out of his room.

Andres had just sat there, grinning like a peacock.

Shaking my head, I frowned at the ache in my stomach. I'd been an emotional wreck most of the day, and after using the bathroom, I knew why.

Ugh.

My period was never regular, and when I got it, boy, did I get it. I dug around my drawers until I found my stash of period underwear and donned an enormous pad, swapping my cute jeans for loose flannel pants and a tank top.

Things had been so hot between us in the kitchen, I'd really been looking forward to some smexy times with my husband.

Curse you, Mother Nature.

I was on the pill, which made things a lot more bearable than they'd been when I was a teenager and had first started my menstrual cycle.

It was a natural part of life.

Of womanhood. Of marriage.

But I was still a little embarrassed thinking about how to tell Andres.

We'd had sex every night since we married, so it wasn't like he wasn't going to notice.

Sex, yes. But I woke up most mornings alone. I frowned, thinking about it, and I realized that was something I should ask him.

Like maybe I was doing something wrong to make him leave every morning before I woke up.

Damn.

"Hey, Sammy fell asleep after having me read the same story three times," Andres said, walking into our bedroom and shrugging out of his shirt.

He paused when he saw me standing there, wringing my hands. Head canted to the side, Andres continued to pull off his suit pants.

"Angel? What's wrong?"

"It's nothing, well, ugh, I'm sorry," I murmured, deciding to rush through it. "I know we started something in the kitchen, and I wanted tonight to be special. Trust me, I really did. I even had a whole thing I was going to put on for you, but, well," I stammered.

"Ellie?" he asked, but it sounded more like a command.

"Fine. I'll just say it. I got my period," I blurted.

"Oh, okay. I understand," he said.

For the first time since we married, I watched

him grab a pair of gym shorts from his drawer and tug them on over his naked body.

"I'm sorry. Um, I'm going to go sit in the living room," I said, sighing.

"Why?"

"Cause I feel bloated and sad and I just wanna lay on the couch with a heating pad, eat popcorn, and watch *John Wick*."

"Sounds good to me. Come on," Andres said, offering me his hand.

"What are you doing?" I asked, feeling as though I was walking in slow motion as Andres led me back to the couch right in front of the ridiculously large entertainment center in the living room.

"Uh, I'm going to watch a movie with you," he replied, eyebrow quirked up adorably.

"Why?" I asked, utterly at a loss and completely confused.

"Isn't that what you want to do?"

"Yessss," I whispered.

"Okay. Let's do it then. I have all the *John Wick* movies downloaded already," Andres replied.

He turned the lights on their dimmest setting and grabbed a throw blanket from a secret little cubby built into the couch. Then he grabbed the remote and handed it to me.

"Are you sure?" I asked, dropping my stunned butt on the comfy couch.

"I'm sure, Angel. Plus, I make really good popcorn. Go get comfortable. I'll be back in a minute," he said, dropping a kiss on my temple.

Swoon.

Something about him kissing me there, right beside the scar Gary gave me, warmed my heart.

I thought about it for a second, and realized it was a spot he kissed often. Heat filled me. Tenderness, too. Some of it spilled down my cheeks.

By the time he came back with a tray overflowing with goodies, I had the movie locked and loaded, my cheeks wiped, and some of my composure back.

Andres looked at me curiously before he handed me the bowl of delicious smelling popcorn and a bag of peanut M&Ms.

My favorite.

Next, he handed me a heated pad that smelled like lavender, and I sighed, placing it on my abdomen.

"Where did you get this?"

"Oh, I ordered it for you, uh, after you guys moved in. My mom swears by them," he said, a sheepish grin on his handsome face.

Dangerous, thoughtful man.

"Smart lady. I think I like her even more now," I said, and made a mental note to find out what his mom liked so we could get her a whole month's supply of it for her upcoming birthday.

"Do you? Like my mom," he said, and bit his lower lip.

I nodded.

"Of course, I do. She's a good woman. Has to be to have raised you," I replied shyly.

"Oh," he said, and I swore I saw something flash inside that stormy gaze of his.

Like lightning.

"So, would you like a juice box, water, or seltzer?" he asked, holding them up.

"Um, juice box," I said, reaching for it.

But instead of handing it to me, Andres tore off the straw and opened it. He stuck the sharp end through the box, then he held it to my mouth and waited for me to take a sip.

I did.

And it was good.

"Press play, Angel," Andres said, sitting back and wrapping an arm around my shoulder.

I leaned into him, placing the bowl of popcorn and the bag of candy on our laps. The movie started.

My husband squeezed my arm, and I adjusted the

heating pad to where I was cramping on my lower back.

"Okay?" he asked.

"Perfect," I replied.

And it was.

I closed my eyes for a moment, and I came to a decision.

A really important decision.

I decided to trust my gut where Andres was concerned. To take what he offered me—his kindness, his affection, his support—and to hold on to it with both hands.

I was a pretty avid reader, and if there was one mistake heroes and heroines the book world over made time and again, it was that they wasted time.

They didn't listen to their hearts or trust their instincts.

My mind told me this was too fast. I'd already made a mess of my life over a man, and I shouldn't be in a rush to do it again.

But my heart told me Andres wasn't anything like Gary. It told me I could depend on him. That he was trustworthy and dependable.

I decided right then to shut my mind off. To simply enjoy the way Andres spoiled me with popcorn and candy.

I knew it was little more than a simple stay-in movie date. But with it, Andres Ramirez just blew my mind. And I was so there for it.

I felt cracks shaking the foundation of the wall I'd built around my heart, and I closed my eyes as they shattered and crumbled.

Would it really be so bad if I fell for my husband?

The next day, I felt like I was walking on cloud nine.

Every time I found myself daydreaming about my sexy AF hubby, I had to stop and do a reality check.

Making me snacks and cuddling me on the couch while binge watching my favorite Keanu Reeves series already catapulted Andres into *quite a catch category*.

But he didn't stop there. Oh no.

The man with a thousand ripples and curves who seemed made of pure muscle carried me to bed after I fell asleep against his side. I hoped I didn't snore. But back to the important bit.

He. Carried. Me.

Lifted my chunky dead-to-the-world ass off the sofa like I weighed nothing at all and brought me to bed. The only reason I knew it for a fact was because I woke up a little when he placed me on the mattress.

"How'd I get here? I'm too heavy to carry," I mumbled, *frowning, and trying to understand how I got there.*

"Not for me. Your body is perfect. You were made for me, Angel," he whispered, *kissing my lips and tucking me in.*

Danger. Danger. DANGER.

How was I supposed to hold on to my heart with him doing and saying stuff like that?

It was impossible. And I wasn't sure I even wanted to.

Good thing Destiny invited me out for dinner with her and the girls. I really needed a break from my hot-as-hell and thoughtful-as-fuck husband, so I accepted.

"Shit," I mumbled.

As if on cue, Rocky, the little minx, zoomed past me. He must have been hiding in the closet again. For some reason, the silly animal loved to linger in the dark.

Still, I smiled, noting with pleasure the allergy meds Andres got for me were doing their job.

Not an accidental sneeze pee incident in sight. Huzzah!

I'd been trying on some of the new blouses Andres had gifted to me, and I was stunned by how amazing his choices were.

Everything was the perfect size, and the designer used materials that were the perfect combination of comfortable and sturdy, but still light and airy. It was as if he could read my mind and knew exactly what I liked.

He was always surprising me, that man.

I slid into a pair of thick, stretchy pants that were super comfortable and stylish.

The blouse was sleeveless and was made of several layers of sheer black fabric so soft and delicate it was like wearing nothing.

If I pulled the layers apart, they were completely see through, but together, I was decently covered.

The scoop neck was a little low, but my boobs were average, so it wasn't indecent. I loved it because of the way the fabric moved and flowed. It was light and not constricting at all. Plus, it hid my stomach, which was what I wanted.

Biting my lip, I wondered if it was too much or too little for a dinner in Manhattan. I shook my head. I was going out with friends, and their wardrobe was undoubtedly filled with designs from the same boutique.

Satisfied with my choice, I finished getting ready. A night with the girls seemed like just the thing.

I felt kind of guilty for going out when Sammy was still awake, but Andres had assured me he would be fine.

Andres really was something. Every time I thought I had him pegged, he surprised me.

I worried he might try to control me or try to stop me from going.

Nope.

On the contrary, Andres was supportive and encouraging. He even seemed happy for me.

"You look gorgeous, Angel," a deep voice interrupted my inner musings, and I jumped.

"Andres! You're home," I said, smiling shyly at my husband.

Holy fuck.

He looked good. Like better than any normal man should after work.

His beard was neat, but his hair was mussed, like he'd been running his fingers through it. His blue-gray irises seemed brighter than normal as he watched me, his arms crossed and one hand on his chin.

"Yeah, I'm *home*," he said, emphasizing the last word as he dropped his arms.

Those stormy eyes I was learning to read ran over me from head to toe. They glittered with approval, and something more.

I decided I was glad I chose that blouse. My cheeks burned, and I felt all shivery inside.

How could I still be shy around this man?

He'd seen, touched, even tasted more of me than any other human being in the whole world. And yet, I was practically trembling with nerves.

"Um, do you mind that I'm going out?" I asked, wanting to know the truth.

"Of course not, Lupina. But you will be safe. Right?"

I nodded.

Of course I would.

"And you won't do anything dangerous."

I shook my head.

Of course I wouldn't.

Plus, I wanted to please him. I knew it was silly of me. But I did.

He approached me, a full blown smile on his face, and took me by the waist. Carefully, slowly, with his eyes on mine, Andres wrapped me up in a hug.

And damn, it felt good. Almost too good.

I smiled with my cheek pressed against his chest, liking the way he seemed made for this.

He was made to hug me.

Growing up the way I did, affection was doled out stingily. We weren't a family who readily embraced.

But living with Andres, I was getting used to his constant touches and the steady stream of admiration, praise, respect, and companionship.

"Good. I trust you and the ladies will have an awesome time," he said, smiling as he dropped a soft kiss on my temple and let me go.

Swoon.

If Andres had asked me to stay home right then, I would have. Without question, I would have.

Knowing that he wouldn't ask that of me. That he would never ask me not to go have dinner with my friends. Well, that just made me more determined to please him.

It made me like him just a little bit more.

Shit.

Truth was, I more than liked him.

It wasn't my fault. He was just so, *so much.*

How could one man be so damn understanding?

So sweet?

So sexy?

I had no idea.

But since he was my man, I was going to accept it. More than that, I was going to revel in it.

What else could I do?

I didn't want to deny my feelings.

For the first time ever, I felt safe, cherished, and protected. They were good feelings, and he was responsible for them.

Andres was a force to be reckoned with, and if I were being honest with myself, I would admit I just didn't want to resist anymore.

The man swept me off my feet.

Literally.

In spite of everything I had been through, it was time to face the very real probability that I was already in love with my husband.

"Okay boys, I'm leaving," Ellie said, entering the living room, which was liberally covered in building blocks, race cars, and kitten toys.

I was sitting on the floor, criss-cross applesauce, helping Sammy build a track, while simultaneously distracting Rocky from destroying the thing, when my wife walked in.

My heart squeezed.

My stomach flipped.

My pants grew tight.

I'd seen her outfit already. Knew what she had on. But for some reason, watching her enter the living room was something else entirely.

It was like watching a shooting star fall right out of the sky.

She stole my breath, dressed in black from head to toe.

Like a midnight goddess.

Mysterious. Ethereal. So fucking sexy.

Fuck.

My cock thumped in my pants, and I leaned forward to make it less noticeable.

My Lupina's pants were so fucking tight, showing every glorious curve like she'd been dipped into them. The flowy top had a deep scoop neck that showed off her sexy-as-fuck cleavage.

When she moved, it moved with her, layers of soft-looking black fabric showing tantalizing glimpses of skin and the lacy black bra she wore beneath it.

She looked gorgeous. She looked like mine.

Whatever womanly magic she'd performed after I'd left the room—you know, those finishing touches females did that seemed to make them glitter and glow from head to toe, those womanly secrets that softened features and emphasized beauty, you get it—well, Ellie did some of that.

And the results left me breathless.

"Ellie," I said, needing to touch her before she left. I jumped to my feet.

"Yeah?" she asked, eyes wide.

"Be careful tonight. Call me if you need anything," I said, moving across the room to cup her face in my hands.

"I will," she smiled, and leaned her head back, kissing me goodbye.

"Bye, Mommy!" Sammy shouted, scrambling to his feet so he could get a kiss too.

I didn't blame him. He ran into our knees, hugging us both, and I grinned before scooping him up so he could snuggle his mom one more time before she went out for her girlfriend dinner.

"Be good, Sweetie," she said, her eyes going round as she hugged him tight.

I knew she was having misgivings, but I wanted her to trust that he would be fine here with me.

"Michael is driving you, and Eduardo will be your bodyguard," I told her, walking her to the door as Sammy chased Rocky around the room.

I grinned as he skipped back over to the race-track we were building and started lining up his cars, having already forgotten about his block tower.

"Oh, I don't need a bodyguard to go to a restau-rant," Ellie said, shaking her head.

"I know you're fierce, Lupina. But you will always have a bodyguard with you when I'm not there, make no mistake."

"But will he be noticeable? I mean, that's kind of weird, no?"

Her frown was so cute. I smoothed the line between her eyes and kissed her again. She was so close, I couldn't resist the chance to taste her. Even chastely.

"No. It's not weird. He knows how to do his job. You just have fun with the others, okay? And don't think for a minute they'll be there without their own bodyguards."

"Okay. You are probably right. Um, I'll be back in a few hours. If you need anything or if Sammy does—"

"Angel, Sammy is going to be fine. My mother is coming by with a brand new cartoon movie for him. She's determined to spoil him rotten."

"I'm missing Nancy? Oh no, I'm sorry," she started.

I knew Ellie and my mother had texted a few times. My mom was trying to be unintrusive, but I was so happy they liked each other. I didn't think it mattered, but having Mom approve of my choice to marry Ellie only solidified my resolve that this was the right thing to do.

Even though she was unaware of my little obsession with her. Or of the fact I'd stalked her from the house down the block when she was in Morristown. Or that I'd hacked her personal files—okay, fine. There was a lot she didn't know.

But it didn't matter. I'd do it all over again if it meant I ended up with her.

Ellie brought a level of satisfaction to me, to the depths of my soul, I never even thought was possible.

Marrying her was better than winning the lottery. But it was that same kind of extreme happiness.

Fuck. She makes me so damn happy.

"It's okay. She's not going anywhere. You'll have plenty of opportunities to hang out with Mom, trust me," I told her and kissed her nose, just because I could.

"Go have some fun, Angel. We'll be here."

"Okay," she said, nodding.

"Text me when you get there, so I know you're safe."

"Okay, I will," she promised, and my chest felt tight.

I walked her to the elevator and watched as she got in the car with her bodyguard. Then I texted Josef, and he confirmed what I already knew.

Adrik had reserved a private room for them in the back of the mid-sized Mediterranean bistro they were going to. The place was one of those New York hotspots that was impossible to get into.

Well, impossible if you weren't a Volkov.

The place was said to serve excellent food and cocktails, and the waiting list was months long. It was all over social media as the place to be, and on some nights, like tonight, they had live music.

I imagined it would be packed. And it made me jumpy.

I couldn't help my protective instincts. Whenever Ellie wasn't with me, I worried. It was just who I was.

But considering my wife's three best friends were some of the best-guarded women in the state, if not the whole damn country, I couldn't think of anyplace safer.

Except by my side.

"Dad! Rocky is eating my cars," Sammy shouted from the living room, and I jogged back inside the room to watch my boy giggling over his silly pet's antics.

"Maybe Rocky needs treats," I said, and Sammy ran to the little box of cat snacks we kept on a low shelf near the front door.

Ten minutes later, my mother arrived, bearing gifts. Sammy adored cartoons. Add that to the homemade double chocolate chip cookies my mother brought with her, and she had a fan for life.

"Can I have another cookie, Nana?" Sammy asked, completely smitten with his new grandmother.

"Of course you can. Don't forget to drink your milk, then we'll get into your jammies and put the movie on," she replied gently.

"Thanks, Mom," I said, standing next to her.

"Oh, Andres, I should thank you. You gave me a new daughter and a built-in grandson."

"Sammy is fantastic, isn't he?" I replied with a smile.

"He is. And he loves you, anyone can see that."

"Do you think so?" I asked, my vulnerability showing.

"Sweetie, I know so. And I am so happy for you. I wondered if you would ever find the right woman. But now I see it wasn't a woman you were waiting for. It was a family. You did good, son."

"It feels that way, Mom. Ellie and Sammy, they

feel so right in here," I whispered, placing a hand over my heart,

"You love her very much, don't you?"

I nodded, the words choking me. It didn't feel right to say it to my mother before I said it to Ellie. But I couldn't lie to her either.

"Good. That woman needs you. And so does this boy. You were born to be a father," Mom said.

"You know, I have to admit I was terrified of being a father. But I learned from good people."

"You think I'm a good mom?" Mom asked me, tears filling her familiar eyes.

"I think you're a damn good mom," I told her, kissing her cheek.

"Thank you. You know, parenting is the easy part. You just love them. Like me and your dad did with you," she said, grinning at Sammy.

My dad.

I smiled as memories of the warm, loving man who'd raised me filled my head. Oh, he wasn't a pushover. There were times I'd needed discipline, and he doled it out with a firm, but loving hand.

No hitting. But he called me on my shit. Made me accountable. Made sure I knew how my actions had consequences.

He passed away far too soon, but I remembered

everything about him. Technically, my mom's husband was my stepfather, but he raised me.

Paolo Ramirez was my dad in every sense of the word, and I couldn't have asked for a better man to do the job.

Together, my mom and I saw to it Sammy brushed his teeth and changed into his little superhero pajamas. We cozied up in the living room, and a half an hour into the flick, the poor little guy was snoozing on my mom's lap.

"I think that's all she wrote for this little champ," my mother said, grinning as she kissed Sammy's sweet head.

"Mm, we should get him in bed," I said, my gaze flicking back to my phone.

I scrolled through the last two texts Ellie sent me. One was to say she'd arrived, and the other was a photo of her dinner.

It looked good. But not as good as her.

"I can put him to bed, son. Why don't you go join that pretty wife of yours?"

My pulse raced, and I canted my head to the side. Leave it to Mom to know I was thinking about doing just that.

"I'm trying not to overwhelm her. Don't want her to think I'm controlling her," I confessed.

I only ever told my mom the truth.

I mean, anyone who had a mother worth a dime knew they were special people. Moms figured out all your secrets, anyway. No matter how hard you tried to hide.

I learned that pretty early in life. So, I didn't bother with lies. Not to her.

"Could be she's missing you, too," Mom said.

And that was just the push I needed to go check on her.

"You sure you're okay watching him?"

"You know I can still kick your ass, right? Get outta here," she teased.

Twenty minutes later, I hopped out of the car, not waiting for the driver to come to a complete stop. I was so amped up, missing my wife, I almost ran right smack into a huge, somehow-familiar back.

"Motherfucker," a teasing voice said from behind me.

"Ha! You too, huh?" I whispered, almost embarrassed, but not quite.

"Look at you three menaces to society. Couldn't even leave your wives alone for a few hours," Josef said at last, shaking his head.

I couldn't stop grinning as I swung my head left

and right, taking in the big bastards standing beside me.

"Uh, in case it skipped your notice, you're here, too, fuckhead," Marat said.

"Who you calling a fuckhead?" Josef grumbled, tugging on his collar.

"Knock it off. Let's find our wives," Adrik grumbled.

"Yeah. Let's find our wives," I seconded.

The air felt charged with masculinity, and I nodded my head, finally feeling like a real part of this quartet. If there was one thing we all had in common, it was the compulsion to be with our women.

It was like a magnetic pull. An unseen force that held us spellbound and unable to resist.

Who would even want to?

I felt more myself with Ellie than with anyone else. She made the bad parts go away.

The loneliness.

The doubt.

The noise.

Ellie was my safe harbor. She filled me with unrepentant joy, and a love so profound I could hardly voice it.

I hadn't voiced it. And I was beginning to think I needed to rectify that.

Adrik led the way with Marat behind him, then me, then Josef. Once a bodyguard, always a bodyguard, I supposed.

Whatever.

I could handle myself. But it was something knowing those big bastards were with me.

Not that there were active threats around or inside the restaurant. If there were, one of the twenty guards we had on the place, keeping our wives safe, would have told us.

Heads swiveled in our direction and dozens of pairs of eyes watched us as we walked past the full tables. We must have looked like a fucking hit squad or something.

The four of us were uncommonly tall and built. I could imagine what regular folks thought. All four miens were serious, unsmiling. We wore dark suits with matching determined expressions as we traipsed through that posh-as-fuck restaurant.

But they could look all they wanted. I didn't give a fuck. I didn't spare them a glance.

I had a one track mind, and right now, it was on my wife. Ellie was close, and my fingers itched to touch her.

A shiver of awareness slithered through me. It was that pull, that magnetic force that always seemed stronger the closer I was to her.

My heart pounded.

My blood sizzled.

I clenched my jaw, working to keep my hands loose at my sides.

My eyes looked forward, my feet kept moving, and I shouldered my way past the throng of restaurant goers standing at the bar, waiting for their turn to eat at the exclusive restaurant.

Turning sideways, keeping pace, I slipped between tables, and followed Adrik's broad motherfucking back as he ducked through a doorway that had a little plaque with the word *private* scrawled across it.

Finally, I saw her. A wide smile was spread across her face, and she looked so damn beautiful my heart ached. Then her gaze flicked to mine, and the whole world stilled.

It was like the air had been sucked out of the room. Everyone else faded to the background. Thunder roared in my ears and my lungs burned, desperate for salvation.

Ellie moved first. She blinked slowly and that smile she wore changed from simply pleasant to absolute joy. And just like that, I could breathe again.

Fuck.

I needed this woman so much.

Did she know? Could she tell?

Ellie was everything right with this fucked up world. And she was mine.

My Lupina.

few minutes earlier...

"Wait, so you mean to tell me Andres hasn't started the whole *twenty questions every time you get up to pee* thing like the rest of them?" Sofia asked, giggling as she sipped some wine mixed with lemon lime soda.

"What do you mean?" I asked.

"Well, she just means the whole possessive vibe the boys have," Meredith explained, rubbing her slight baby bump.

"Possessive vibe?"

"Yeah, like when you're in bed and he's all like *tell me you are mine, show me you want me or no orgasm for you,*" Destiny said in what had to be the worst male voice ever.

I almost choked on my drink.

I couldn't remember the last time I'd laughed so hard. Or ate so much.

Goddamn.

Everything was amazing.

The food.

The drinks.

The women.

The jokes.

The laughter.

And it was exactly what I needed.

"Marat does that? I swear to God, if Adrik threatens to withhold my orgasm, I'll kick his ass."

"His fine ass," Meredith added.

"Truth. My husband has a fine ass. As do all our men, I must admit."

I giggled some more. The girls were fantastic about teasing one another and making outrageous comments about each other's men. But it was all in good fun.

There was such a strong bond between them. It made me feel blessed to be included.

We shushed as one of our servers came in with the next course. Apparently, Adrik had reserved a private room for us, a special six course menu, and a slew of servers to see to our needs.

It didn't escape my notice they were all female. And when I remarked on it, the *wives of wolves* just snorted.

"As if they would allow men to wait on us," Destiny said, shaking her head.

"Your husband is one of the hottest guys I've ever seen, you mean he's jealous?" I asked, disbelieving.

"Oh, Marat knows he's a handsome devil, but if you want to talk proprietary, the man is a beast. And I mean that in the best possible way," she told me, and her eyes were sparkling with delight.

"You better be talking about me, Dumplin'," the man himself said, walking into our private dining room bold as brass.

Stunned, my gaze flicked to the doorway where I saw not just Marat, but Adrik, Josef, and, *oh, my ovaries*, Andres, too.

Sexier than anyone had a right to look, he wore a black shirt and a slate gray suit. The top three buttons of his shirt were undone, giving me a tantalizing view of dark chest hair.

I loved that he wasn't one of those men who waxed or shaved or whatever. I liked my man real. And he was as real as it got.

Andres stalked over to my side of the table and my mouth went completely dry. The other men were saying hello to their wives, but I wasn't paying them any mind.

All my attention was on *him*.

My larger-than-life husband.

This man, who seemingly came out of nowhere and swept me off my feet. Who I took one look at and just blindly trusted with mine and Sammy's lives.

Maybe I was a fool.

But there was just something about him that said *don't worry, I got you.*

I just knew he would take care of us. Call it a sixth sense, or just call me a fool. It didn't matter.

I trusted Andres. Even if this was the first time, I truly admitted that to myself.

I'd had bad and mean and rough. I'd been married to a man who saw me as little more than a pawn. Andres was the first man who saw me for me.

He saw all my dark and dirty, all my ugly. And still, he'd said yes.

My heart squeezed so hard, I gasped. Andres frowned, canting his head to the side like he knew exactly what I was feeling.

He was like this big, sturdy oak. A tall, unbreachable tower. A natural born protector, taking me and

Sammy under his wing. Giving us shelter. Keeping us dry and warm.

His hand gripped the back of my neck as he came right next to me, and he crouched down.

"You good, Lupina?"

A hum of contentment moved through my blood as I smiled at him. I lifted my face, and he leaned in, kissing me on the mouth.

Holy. Shit.

Our lips remained closed, but still. It was incredible.

The man could kiss. I was still smiling when he pulled back with one last peck.

"Yes, Husband. I'm perfect."

Four more chairs were brought inside the private room, and our wives made spaces for us.

I worried that maybe it was intrusive of us to just drop in on them, but looking around at how all the women seemed happy to have their husbands join them, I relaxed.

The first thing she'd asked about was Sammy, but after I assured her he was safe and sound and tucked up in bed with my mom as a babysitter, she settled down.

Her trust was humbling.

Hell.

It was everything.

I placed my hand on her thigh, loving that she

didn't flinch or shy away from the touch as I leaned down to brush my lips across her temple, kissing the scar that wore like a badge of honor.

She was so brave.

So strong.

I hated that she was ever hurt. Ever scared.

But I loved how she leaned on me, how she had faith in me despite all she'd been through.

I would never let her down. I'd make it my life's work to give her and Sammy the life they deserved. One they could be proud of.

Our condo was located inside a building with the best security available. Ellie was aware of at least some of the extra steps I took to ensure the safety of my small but precious family.

Maybe Ellie wasn't in love with me yet. But she smiled at me, and she scooted her chair over so I could sit beside her. And even now, she melted into my side as I draped an arm around her shoulder.

"Was everything good?"

"Oh, yeah. Delicious. Are you hungry?"

"Nah. My mom stuffed me and Sammy with cookies before bed," I told her, grinning sheepishly.

"Did you save any for me?" she asked, and I narrowed my eyes.

"No, I figured you'd have some fancy dessert here."

"Come here," she said.

"Why?"

"Cause I want to taste those cookies," she whispered.

Then my shy, sweet, adorable wife shocked the shit out of me and kissed me in front of everyone.

This wasn't the same close-lipped kiss I'd given her upon arrival. This was different. It was lips and tongues and teeth.

I ignored the wolf whistles and the applause. Too caught up in the feel of her plump lips working against mine.

Slowly, she withdrew her mouth, eyes sparkling with mischief, and my heart thudded heavily in my chest.

"Good?" I asked.

"So good."

Heat filled me, and she turned her attention to some story Marat was animatedly telling. But she leaned her weight against my side, and I breathed in her warm scent as a feeling of rightness settled deep inside my soul.

I couldn't believe she was really there with me.

Like really with me. But she was. And it was fantastic. Better than I imagined.

Ellie was my missing link. That missing piece to my puzzle that made me whole.

The second I saw her, I knew she was the one. So, I did what anyone in my position would do.

I inserted myself into her life.

Okay, I fucking stalked her.

But only with the best intentions.

I fantasized about her, for sure.

But never once in all my planning, plotting, and dreaming did I think she would so readily thrust herself into my arms.

It was the greatest honor of my life.

"I think I'm ready to go home," she whispered an hour later, after everyone had their coffee or after dinner drink.

Just the fact she used that word sent my soul to singing.

Home.

"Yeah? Good. I'm ready, too."

So fucking ready.

A few days had passed since our night out. Andres had been working crazy hours, and even though he came home for dinner every night, he went back to the office right after.

I tried to ask him what he was working on, and he told me not to worry. He was taking care of it.

Dread filled me. I knew it must have had something to do with Gary and his lawsuits.

One after the other, they came every day in the mail. The bastard was suing me for just about everything.

Mine and Sammy's trust funds. My inheritance. Maxwell Mining. Alimony. The condo where he lived.

But the worst of it was, of course, his suit for visitation rights and sole custody of Sammy.

I'd give Gary all of my possessions and money if he would just go away. But he wouldn't.

I knew him well enough to know he got his real kicks off of control. That man was a demon, and not in any good or sexy kind of way.

He was evil. And vile. And I hated him.

I closed my eyes, hand on my stomach. I hated confrontations. And this was one I'd been alternately dreading and looking forward to. I mean, I wanted to get it over with. But I was so afraid.

Afraid to lose my son.

Afraid to put him in harm's way.

The meeting with Gary and his lawyers had been pushed to this evening, and my nerves were shot.

"Get it together, Ellie," I told myself, staring at my reflection inside mine and Andres' bathroom.

The first part of any battle was preparing for it, or so I'd been told. In this case, preparations included dressing the part.

Gary was a stickler for perfection, and I knew he would be in one of his custom three piece suits tailored to fit his thin body.

His white hair would be slicked back, not a

strand out of place, and I imagined he'd be drenched in that godawful cologne he wore. He had his hair trimmed every nine days like clockwork.

He never had facial hair. Honestly, I didn't even know if he could grow any.

Those cold, lackluster eyes would be ready to zero in on anything he deemed faulty, which was usually anything having to do with me.

He never wore even a trace of emotion on his pale face other than disdain. And I wondered for the first time if he felt anything for anyone besides himself.

Chauvinist pig.

I really didn't know what I ever saw in Gary Peters. He wasn't anything like the kind of man I liked.

But maybe that was because I only discovered what I liked recently.

It seemed I had a penchant for bronzed skin stretched over too many muscles to count, dark chest hair, and sexy tattoos. I also liked facial hair and dark, stormy eyes, lips that were made to kiss, and big, powerful hands that knew just how to hold a woman my size.

Amen.

Of course, I was daydreaming about my husband.

He was the sexiest man I'd ever seen. Certainly, the hottest one who ever wanted anything to do with me.

He did want me.

There was no denying that.

Andres' attention hadn't wavered even after my clumsy argument with him a few nights ago.

Having to admit I got my period right after our little tiff was mortifying, but he made it all seem so easy.

Getting me a heating pad, making snacks for us to share, and cuddling with me on the couch while we watched Keanu Reeves avenge the murder of the puppy his late wife gifted him was just the most perfect night.

I'd felt cherished, cared for, and that was new. The things he said and did that night and every night since had left me feeling slightly confused, and more than a little hopeful.

His reaction to Sammy calling him Dad had the walls around my heart cracking just a little bit more.

Okay, fine.

That wall had split wide fucking open.

The man was undoing every precaution I ever

took to make sure this thing between us didn't get messy. But I had a feeling I was too late for that.

The way I felt about Andres was new and sweet, but also scary. I was so attracted to him. It was like a signal went off inside my body whenever he was within ten feet of me.

I wanted him with a fervor that was borderline manic.

After my period subsided, I'd let him know subtly.

Or maybe not so subtly.

He came home for dinner, and instead of grabbing my comfy flannel pants while he changed to head back to the office as he had been doing most nights this week, I followed him into the bedroom after tucking Sammy in for the night.

Andres was standing just inside the walk-in closet, and I closed our bedroom door with a soft click.

Then I pulled off my jeans and t-shirt. In nothing but my black cotton panties and matching bralette, I entered the closet. Andres' heated gaze found mine, and a sharp exhale left his lips.

I'd never done anything like that, and I was so damn nervous.

What if he thought I was being too forward? What if I grossed him out?

I wanted him so badly.

Hell.

I needed him.

But I wasn't sure I could bring myself to say the words. So I stripped instead, hoping he got the picture.

A split second later, he was on me. All my inhibitions fled as my sexy-as-fuck husband crushed me to him, kissing me with a fervor that sent tingles shooting through every nerve ending.

It was the first night I didn't reach for him first. At least, not physically.

And I was so ready for him. Even just a few days of abstinence were too much. My pussy felt so empty without him filling me. Arousal dripped from my lips, soaking my panties.

"Need you, Lupina. Missed you," he growled, his hands *fisting in my hair.*

"Andres," I whimpered.

"God, you taste so good. The perfect combination of sweetness and sin," he murmured, catching my lower lip *between his teeth, and biting me.*

I remembered gasping, clutching at his shoulders.

We were like two wild things, pushed together by

some unseen force. Unable and unwilling to even try to fight it.

Now that I knew why he called me Lupina and what it meant, I had to admit it was a real turn on for me.

Andres didn't want me to be weak. Or cowed. He wanted me to be strong. He liked my ferocity, and I was goddamn feral for him.

Chills raced up my spine, making me tremble. No one had ever admired my strength before.

No one had ever even noticed it. But Andres had.

He noticed, and he thought it was sexy as fuck.

Gulp.

Oh, I was in so much trouble with that man.

It shouldn't have been a turn on. All that muted violence shouldn't have made my heart race and my body shiver with need, but it did.

I wanted him so damn bad.

And like always, all he had to do was touch me and I turned into a puddle of need.

"Get on your knees, Wife, and open that fucking mouth," he growled, and I obeyed.

Falling to my knees should have felt submissive. But with him, I felt like a goddess. I grabbed his cock with my hand and parted my lips, sucking on the thick head.

"Fuck," he groaned.

Andres held my head in place and pushed his length down my throat.

I'd never had a dick in my mouth before. And I gagged around his girth.

Andres made noises that sounded like pure lust, and they encouraged me. So I tried again, sucking him down as far as I could.

On and on for long minutes, I sucked and licked, and fucked my husband with my mouth. His words of encouragement made me feel bold. Made me feel beautiful.

He allowed me a few more strokes before he dragged his dick out of my mouth and pulled me to my feet.

"Nuh uh. I'm coming inside your cunt tonight, Wife."

Then he pushed me back onto the bed and lifted my legs, so my calves were sitting on his shoulders.

Andres' hands moved to my thighs, and he held me open. My pussy and ass cheeks both.

He rubbed his dick along my dripping seam, making us both moan when he brushed the tip along my puckered hole.

"Gonna fuck this ass, Lupina. Not tonight, but soon," he told me, sending another wave of desire roaring through me.

Then he shoved all the way inside me, using one hand to pinch my throbbing clit as he pressed deeper than ever before, and I fell apart.

Andres made me come two more times before he was through, and every time he fed his dick to my pussy, I felt as though he were putting all the broken pieces of me back together.

And I didn't know how to handle that.

Healthy relationships were built on more than sex.

Everyone said so.

Logically, I knew there must be some truth in that statement.

But there was something to be said for physically connecting with someone. In my not-expert opinion, sex sated more than carnal appetites, it brought people closer.

Having sex with Andres was an intimacy I'd never shared with anyone else, and it made me feel closer to him. It boosted my energy, my confidence, my happiness.

But maybe that was just him. He was so supportive. Easily the kindest, most sincere man I'd ever met.

Andres had been insatiable for me that night. And every night since. I reciprocated that feeling.

And then some.

I wanted the man all the time. Like, all the time. So much so, I actually used the little clitoral massage toy Sofia had bought me as a bachelorette party present, even though I didn't have a bridal shower.

Note to self. Tell Sofia a thank you when I see her.

I swallowed down my lusty thoughts. There was no way I wanted to go to this lawyer's meeting thinking about sex with my fine as fuck man.

After I brushed my teeth, I turned the water on inside the stupid luxurious shower of the main bathroom that was attached to mine and Andres' bedroom.

Stepping beneath the stream of hot water, I sighed, allowing the constant stream to wash away some of my stress.

I knew the meeting with Gary was going to be horrible.

Everything with Gary was horrible.

And I wished I could say that was why I was freaking out.

On some level, it was, of course. I was so worried

that bastard would somehow win visitation with Sammy, and I knew I could never allow it.

But my stress was due to something else. Something totally unexpected.

I think I might be desperately in love with my husband.

Every time I thought I had his motivations defined, Andres took me by surprise.

Like when he came home to eat dinner with us every night. Like we were a real family. That was one of the first and biggest shocks I'd had to contend with after Sammy and I moved into Andres' condo.

I was going to miss that tonight, but of course, Gary's lawyers had asked to meet during the time I usually set for Sammy, and now all of us, to have our evening meal.

Gary would have remembered that. And he would have chosen the time on purpose.

Dick.

What he did not know was my new husband had no problem leaving work a couple of hours early, just so Sammy could still enjoy dinner with the two of us.

Thoughtful man.

Dangerous man.

The man was terrifying. And I didn't mean Gary.

I meant Andres.

My husband.

Didn't he know it was dangerous doing things like that? That it was terrifying to make me wonder if I had real feelings for him? Even worse, to make me want them.

How could I keep what we were doing in check if he went around confusing me like that?

I exited the shower, rubbing lotion on my skin and a thick-toothed comb through my hair. I applied my face cream and some texturizing hair product to make my bouncy curls behave while I let them air dry.

After our early dinner, Andres excused himself.

He had to head back to Volkov Towers, promising to meet me at the law firm where Gary's lawyers were hosting this little meeting.

He was going to send a car to get me from Josef's security firm. And we'd already borrowed Nanny Rosa from Sofia and Adrik to sit with Sammy while we were gone.

I didn't feel comfortable hiring our own nanny just yet, and Andres was not forcing the issue.

In fact, the only time he brought it up was when we first moved in. That was about the same time he said I didn't have to cook or clean or anything. That he would hire any staff I needed or wanted.

But I enjoyed cooking, and Andres seemed to like eating whatever I made well enough.

Danger.

Andres was an enigma to me. I'd never known a man like him. But I wanted to. I found myself wanting to know everything about him.

What made him tick?

What did he like?

What did he want?

What did he need?

I wanted to know it all. He gave me so much, and I really had no clue what, if anything, I did for him.

I didn't feel indebted. Not like I had to pay him back. No. It wasn't like that.

But I did want to do something, *anything*, for him. I applied some light cosmetics and pulled on my underthings without haste.

Dressing in privacy and at my own leisure were luxuries I'd missed. When I was staying at St. Elizabeth's, the bathrooms were communal, and even though the Morristown house offered privacy, it hardly compared to this.

But I knew that had more to do with the way I felt inside.

I'd been scared and facing this on my own back then. Now I had people in my corner. I had Meredith, Des, and Sof, and the support of their husbands. I had Nancy, my sweet mother-in-law, who texted me often. I had Mrs. Stevens, who'd been so kind to me.

And best of all, I had Andres.

St. E's had been a godsend. That place saved me, and I knew I owed it a debt. It brought me Meredith and my new friends. It brought me Andres.

I'd already decided I would volunteer there when Sammy was in school full time and after we finished dealing with Gary and his cancerous bullshit.

God, I hate him.

I really did. And not just for what he did to me, for laying hands on me and threatening my boy, but for being a total piece of shit weasel of a man.

I used to be terrified of Gary, but there was a part of me now that recognized him for what he was.

An insignificant blight on humanity. A pitiful excuse for a man.

Yes, I was afraid he'd push his claim on my son, but I trusted Andres to deal with it.

Thank God for Andres.

I headed for the walk-in closet and looked at what was my side of the enormous space.

Andres had told me to use it when I first moved in. But my meager belongings hadn't filled even a third of the shelves, drawers, and racks available.

Like he had shown me in so many other ways, Andres understood my discomfort.

There was nothing wrong with flannel pants and sweatshirts, but if I was going to live in his world, I needed something more than the few pieces of clothing I'd managed to collect these past months.

After moving in, as if by magic, I woke up one day to dozens of new articles of clothing, both on hangers and lining the shelves, filling the previously empty spaces.

I'd already blubbered all over him for the amazing things he'd gotten for Sammy. Clothes, toys, the cat condos lining just about every free wall in the place.

Everything was by the same designer as the wedding dresses Andres had sent me. He was just the most thoughtful man.

Tonight was going to be rough, and I needed something staid. I needed to look respectable, but it had to be something that bolstered my confidence.

I moved around, touching hangers and perusing shelves. Each thing was more beautiful than the last, and I was just overwhelmed. Even when I had money, I never dressed that way.

Finding trendy clothing for my plus-sized body was always a challenge. Also, there was the fact I was always trying to live up to someone else's expectations of what I should wear or look like.

I recalled something I read in a magazine article once upon a time and I finally recognized the wisdom of the statement.

Just because it looks good on the mannequin doesn't mean it looks good on you.

Truer words were never spoken, I thought and snorted.

Andres seemed to know exactly what would look good on me. The designer dressed a lot of plus-sized women, and I appreciated the quality and cut of the clothes almost as much as I appreciated my husband purchasing them for me.

Every piece was superb and just what I'd want for myself. It was like Andres had told him I was a mom, someone who liked to cook, and that I kept fairly active.

There were several versatile pieces and activewear, both of excellent quality and durability. But there were fancier articles, too.

Even those were edgier than I'd ever bought for

myself. I bit my lip, excited about clothes for the first time in a very long time.

All the colors were bright and bold. Not soft pastels that made me look washed out.

They suited me, and I bit my lip, grinning at the deep necklines and fitted waists. The one place where his preferred color choice for me, *black*, reigned supreme was in my panty drawer.

"Let's see," I sighed, running my hands over the dozens of silky, lacy confections.

Okay, so Andres certainly knew how to bolster a girl's confidence.

Sweet, sexy man.

I sucked in a deep breath, swapped the plain underwear set I'd put on for one of the new, sexier black lace panties and bra sets that filled my lingerie drawers.

After making sure my new under things were in place and comfy, I grabbed a pair of black, high-waisted, wide-legged pants and paired them with a deep green sweater.

The scoop neck wasn't immodest, but it did marvelous things for my breasts and belly, making the former appear larger than the latter, and making me feel ultra feminine but not wimpy in the slightest.

I pulled on a pair of black ankle boots and used a spritz of my favorite scent. Then I headed to the living room to grab my purse and cell phone.

"Whoa," a deep voice rumbled behind me.

I turned around and slapped a hand to my chest, startled.

"Ooh! Andres! You scared me."

"Sorry, I thought you heard me," he murmured, his eyes glued to my body.

I had to admit, I was flattered. A man like that losing his cool over me?

Whoa, indeed.

"I thought you were going to meet me there," I said, trying to slow my beating heart.

"I was, but I finished my call early," Andres said, his blue-gray eyes raking over me from head to toe.

My whole body tingled beneath his hungry stare.

"Oh, well, good, I'm glad you're home. And thank you."

"What are you thanking me for, Wife?" he asked.

He canted his head to the side in that manner he had, reminding me of a curious animal. My belly warmed, and I bit my lip, gesturing to myself.

"God, for so many things. First, I never thanked you for the clothes," I said, looking down at my new outfit.

"My pleasure," he said, his gaze lingering on my breasts.

"And I never thanked you for marrying me. For dealing with Gary. And my father's company. For protecting Sammy."

"Shh," Andres said, crossing the distance between us.

He cupped my cheeks and kissed my lips, a soft peck before pressing his forehead to mine.

"You never have to thank me for that, Lupina. It's my privilege. All of it. Now, let's go say goodbye to Sammy before we deal with that piece of shit."

"Okay," I agreed, too anxious to argue.

I kissed Sammy goodbye, smiling as he showed me the puzzle he and Nanny Rosa were working on.

Then, watching Andres kneel to admire my son's handiwork, I had to place a hand over my heart that was currently trying to beat me to death.

Sammy, my sweet boy, tossed his arms around my husband's neck and kissed him on the cheek.

"Goodnight, Dad!"

"See ya later, Sweet Boy. Tomorrow is a big day. You remember what it is?"

"The groomer is coming to give Rocky his bath," Sammy said proudly.

"That's right. And she's gonna trim his nails so no more scratches, okay?"

"Yay! Rocky is gonna feel better, too?"

"That's right. Goodnight, Sammy."

"Thanks, Dad. Night."

My eyes filled with happy tears watching the interaction between them, *my two boys*, and yeah, I fell a little deeper, a little harder.

"You good?" Andres asked, frowning at me.

"Yeah," I replied.

I nodded and offered him a bright smile.

Gary didn't know Andres had been a better father over the matter of weeks he'd had with Sammy than Gary had been over the last four years.

Suddenly, I didn't really care what Gary knew.

All that mattered was right there in front of me.

My boys. My son and my husband. The two greatest loves of my life.

Andres was in a completely different league than Gary.

Hell.

I didn't even think they were the same species.

Gary was slime. A piffling blip on my radar that I would've regretted meeting entirely were it not for my son.

And Andres was, *well*, Andres was mine.

For the first time since I said *I do,* I looked at the man I took as my husband, and I allowed that thought to roll around inside my brain.

He's mine.

The question was, what was I going to do with him?

I mean, it was obvious we had chemistry. But did we have more?

My heart pounded a little harder, and my mouth went dry.

"You ready?" he asked, his stormy gaze darting over me.

"What? Oh, um, yes. Is it cold outside?" I asked.

The weather was unpredictable this time of year, and you really couldn't be sure what to wear. It was a valid question.

Even if I felt like a coward because the words I really wanted to say had nothing to do with the weather, and everything about the man and what he was doing to my heart.

He's wrecking me.

"You should bring a jacket or one of those wraps you like, just in case," he murmured, those blue-gray eyes boring into me.

It felt like he was looking right into my soul. Like

I was stripped bare for him, and he knew exactly what he was doing to me.

I shivered and walked to the closet in the front hall and grabbed an oversized scarf that doubled as a pashmina.

It was one I'd had forever. It had belonged to my father's mother or his aunt or something. There were dozens more in my father's home, but this one had been my favorite.

Hopefully, when all of this was over, I could go back and see what I would keep and what I would sell. I hadn't visited my father's house in years. Since his death, it had been closed up, locked away while his will was in probate. And of course, now, with Gary's lawsuits, it would be tied up even longer.

It was soft. Cashmere, I thought, and the paisley print was done in dark greens, cinnamons, and burgundy. It looked good with my outfit.

I listened for Andres' footfalls coming down the hall and waited for him. We rode the elevator in silence, and Andres held the door to our car open for me.

It was far more convenient to use a car service in the city because of the hassles of parking and traffic. The driver was one I recognized, but his eyes stayed forward as Andres slid into the seat beside me.

"Will we be on time?" I asked, gnawing my bottom lip.

"Yes. Don't worry, Lupina. It's going to be okay," he said, placing his large hand on my thigh.

The contact was just what I needed, and instead of pushing him away or freezing, I did something that shocked even myself.

I leaned into him, closing my eyes, and breathing his masculine scent, bolstering myself with his strength and energy.

I felt something warm and firm press against my head, and I sighed. My husband had kissed me on the head.

Gently. Sweetly.

And it was everything I'd always wanted.

Affection. Support. Unwavering strength.

Oh God, I am in love with him.

I didn't dare open my eyes again as we moved like snails through the thick traffic. Rain started pelting against the windows, and I gasped as thunder roared and lightning struck.

"It'll pass, Lupina," Andres whispered, tightening his hold on my leg.

That's what I was afraid of.

That all of this would pass.

I bit my lip and offered a prayer to whoever was listening.

Please keep Sammy safe.

Don't let Gary get his slimy hands on my son.

And please, if it's possible, let me keep Andres.

Let me have this one thing for me. Please.

Tears filled my eyes, and I felt wretched for being so selfish. I had other things to worry about than the possibility that I was so far gone in love with my own husband, I couldn't breathe.

What do I do now?

What do I do if this is too much for him?

What do I do when he wants to leave me?

Panic was seconds away from setting it. But I couldn't afford to have a nervous breakdown. I couldn't pause to think about any of that right then.

I had to focus on the enemy I was about to face. Not the enemy that was my self-doubt.

Get your game face on, Ellie. It's time.

The car ride was ripe with emotions.

Hers and mine.

I was so amped up about her coming face to face with her ex, it was all I could do to keep on breathing.

I was used to pushing myself. To facing uncomfortable situations head on. But I didn't like the idea of Ellie being in the same room as him.

That motherfucker owed me a debt, and I intended to collect.

Just not yet.

Not today.

I had to remind myself of that frequently as the driver maneuvered the crowded streets.

There was the usual rush hour traffic, plus the

dinner crowd out and about on the glittering streets of Manhattan.

I understood the reason behind the sparkly shit. It was a little Mica and Silicarb mixed with the cement and asphalt.

Really, who needed to know all that?

To a kid from Hoboken, New York was still the Big Apple. It was a concrete jungle.

If you could make it there, well, you knew the rest.

I spent my youth staring across the Hudson River. Checking out the city people traveled to from all over the globe.

I always was ambitious.

Fact was the city streets glittered with asphalt and minerals. But I knew it represented magic. And what was magic but possibilities?

That was the heart of New York.

Smoke and mirrors to some, made to dazzle the tourists.

But I wasn't one of them.

I wasn't passing through.

New York City was my home now. And I was a wolf.

A Volkov.

The city was mine.

Ellie and Sammy were mine.

And tonight, I was going to use everything I had to protect what was mine.

I'd worked hard and long to become the man I was today. A man worthy of Ellie and Sammy. A man who could keep them safe and love them the way they deserved to be loved.

I inhaled a deep breath, sucking in the flavors of my wife as she sat still and silent beside me.

I couldn't imagine what was going on inside her brain.

I hoped she would share it with me when she was ready. But I wouldn't force it.

Never that.

The driver pulled up to the curb and exited the vehicle, but I was already opening my door. He knew better than to try to touch the handle on my wife's side.

The driver just stood there, as did the other bodyguard who exited the passenger side of the SUV. I nodded, appreciating their professionalism.

But I expected nothing less from Sigma International. Josef knew what he was doing, and so did those who worked for him.

"Wait there, Angel," I told Ellie, and she nodded.

She didn't know about the meeting I had earlier

with my investigators, her lawyers, and mine. I hadn't told her yet.

Ellie was unaware of the intel I'd gathered on Gary Peters, and his current wife and ex-secretary.

She was also blissfully unaware of the mountain of fabricated accusations Gary intended to slander my wife with at this meeting today.

But I knew about them. And that douchebag wasn't getting the chance to hurl any of his filth at her ever again.

Tonight I was going to reveal what I'd been doing these past few days, putting in all kinds of hours to see it done right.

Tonight, I was going to shut down all the legal bullshit Gary had put into motion, and I was going to force him to back down.

Tomorrow, well, tomorrow was for something else.

Gary didn't have many more tomorrows to worry about.

All I had to do was think about Ellie when I'd first laid eyes on her.

Her pretty face all bruised and bandaged.

Nose out of joint.

Her arm in a cast.

Oh, he was going to fucking pay for that.

I rounded the car and opened her door, holding my hand out to Ellie like I had on our wedding day.

Her golden green gaze met mine, and I held my breath. Watching her like the predator I was until I saw her decide. I exhaled the second she placed her hand in mine.

Then I helped her out of the car, wrapping one arm around her lower back.

I kissed her once. A hard, quick peck on her mouth just because I could.

"Do you trust me?" I asked.

"Yes," she said, and I nodded.

Ellie said she trusted me, and I had to believe her. I had no choice. I just hoped to God she fucking meant it, because my wife wasn't going to like what I was about to do.

I supposed the office was just like every other law firm in New York.

Professional. Impersonal. Tidy, but still opulent. Boring, yet intimidating.

I rubbed my sweaty hands on my slacks and hugged my pashmina closer to me as I entered the elevator with Andres and the bodyguard we brought with us.

Eduardo, I believed, was his name. The same guy who came with me to the restaurant when I met the girls out for dinner. He ignored me, and I was happy to return the favor. I was too nervous to make small talk.

Andres placed his hand against the small of my

back, and I leaned into him, grateful for his strength and support.

I knew my husband was a man with a wealth of resources at his fingertips, but I didn't know how much he knew about Gary.

My ex was a slimy sonofabitch, but he was smart when he was determined.

"Mr. and Mrs. Ramirez? They are waiting for you inside," an older woman with short, gray hair greeted us when we exited the elevator.

She pointed to a conference room on the other side of the hall, and I faltered a step. My feet felt glued to the floor.

"It's okay," Andres murmured, and I relaxed instantly.

Of course, Gary and his new wife were already inside. The new Mrs. Peters—her first name I didn't know, or if I did know it at one point, I couldn't remember it, and really, I didn't care to—sat with her back ramrod straight.

She was wearing a pristine Chanel suit in a fall appropriate pink with gold accents and her blonde hair twisted back in a neat chignon.

She didn't look at me.

But when I looked closer, I saw the telltale signs

of faint bruising on her cheek. Emotion filled me, twisting my gut. She'd done an excellent job of covering up the greens and blues of her injuries with cosmetics.

But I knew what she was hiding. I used to hide, too. I remembered it all. The disbelief, the fear, the guilt. I swallowed, pushing those awful emotions back down.

My heart went out to her, and to everyone like her.

Everyone like me.

Well, the me I used to be. I wished for a better world. Where women who had suffered at the hands of someone bigger, stronger, and meaner than them knew their true worth. Found the help they needed. And the support to get to a better place.

I was lucky. I knew that, and I was so fucking grateful.

No man should ever raise his hands to a woman.

It was a physical contest whose outcome was already predetermined by biological design. It wasn't fair or right.

Sure, there were women who could kick a man's ass. I didn't doubt that. And I wasn't arguing that point.

But I couldn't think of a single instance where a wife or girlfriend deserved to be hit.

The same went for the reverse.

I'd heard of men who'd suffered abuse at the hands of their spouses and girlfriends.

Either way, it didn't matter.

Violence towards your mate was not okay.

If you didn't want to be with someone, just leave. You didn't have to cheat, lie, manipulate, or hit.

You never had to hit.

Those were just lies.

Vile means used by small, weak, scared people to try to make themselves feel better about their pathetic existences.

Anyone who said you deserved to be cheated on, lied to, hit, or abused in any way, shape, or form were the real liars. Those were just lame ass excuses to be miserable human beings, spreading pain and despair because of their own feelings of worthlessness.

I knew that now. I understood that better than most.

Suddenly, I wanted to cross the room.

I wanted to go to Gary's new wife and tell her she didn't have to stay with him.

She wouldn't look at me, though. Hell, she wasn't looking anywhere but down.

My throat tightened, and suddenly, I didn't give two shits about Gary, except to hate him a little more.

I just wanted to make sure this woman, *his wife*, knew she didn't deserve the way he treated her.

No one deserved that.

"Late as usual," Gary hissed, and I froze with affronted anger.

"Are we?" Andres said, the hand on my back subtly pulled on my waistband, stopping me in my tracks.

"By seven minutes," Gary replied.

"My apologies, Gar. But you know women," my husband said, offering a jovial smile to my ex.

I did a double take.

What the actual fuck?

Why was my husband grinning like a madman and offering Gary his hand like they were fucking buddies?

"Indeed," Gary said, his expression cautious.

But he couldn't hide the flash of disgust in his cold eyes.

"Greetings Mr. Ramirez, I'm Mr. Orion, representing Mr. and Mrs. Peters," a small thin man with a wire-thin mustache introduced himself.

He looked harmless, but I knew Gary, and that meant this lawyer was a fucking shark.

"Yes, yes, Orion, let's just get down to it, shall we?" Mr. O'Doyle, my attorney, interrupted.

"Yes, well, Mrs. Maxwell-Peters, it seems with your recent address change my client has not been able to contact his son. Also, there is a question of your rights in taking him—"

"Ramirez," Andres growled the word.

"Pardon?" Mr. Orion asked.

"Her name is Ellie Ramirez," Andres corrected the lawyer, the smile on his face looking a little more feral than jovial.

I didn't dare look at him closely.

I was caught between confusion and rage. I didn't understand what Andres was playing at.

One minute, he was acting like he actually liked Gary. But the next minute, I swore I could feel masculine energy rolling off him in waves.

"Uh, yes. *Mrs. Ramirez*, my apologies. As I was saying, your recent address change is not on file and your kidnapping of my client's son—"

"Kidnapping? That's a joke, right?" I barked, but

Andres squeezed my thigh beneath the table, silencing me.

"Her recent address change has not been imparted to your client because of my high profile job. My residence is not public knowledge as it would create security risks, I am sure you understand," Andres said, and all hints of friendliness vanished.

"Mr. O'Doyle, perhaps you should explain to your client that he should refrain from speaking, especially since he can also be charged with the kidnapping of a minor child," Mr. Orion spat.

Gary's expression turned smug, and my stomach twisted again.

I felt sick.

Kidnapping?

Could he really threaten us with that?

"Excuse me," Andres said, and there it was.

I could almost see it happening.

The shift.

The change.

No more sweet, attentive husband. This Andres was the badass businessman so many people spoke about when we first met.

"There seems to be a misunderstanding."

"Mr. Ramirez, I insist you refrain from speaking.

Mr. O'Doyle Please tell your client—" Mr. Orion tried again, the worm of a man grinning like he was going to get something over on Andres.

I almost felt bad for him.

Almost.

Whatever Andres was up to, I was sure this wasn't going to end well. I only hoped I was on the winning side, but I didn't understand what he was doing.

He kept me in the dark. And I hated it.

"First, I am not Mr. O'Doyle's client. And I am here for my wife and my son," Andres said, emphasis on the last bit.

There was a pause as all the attention in the room shifted to my husband.

"Um, I'm confused. We are here to discuss the issue of visitation concerning the minor child, Samuel Maxwell-Peters," Mr. Orion said, reading Sammy's name off a sheet of paper.

It was probably the first time he had ever read my son's name, and just knowing that increased my fury.

"No, I believe you are mistaken. Our business concerns Maxwell Mining, doesn't it, Gary?" Andres asked, his stormy eyes darker than I'd ever seen them.

"What do you have to do with the company?" Gary scoffed.

"Didn't you know? I just signed the deal this afternoon. I am the sole owner of Maxwell Mining," Andres said, silencing everyone in the room.

My heart was pounding.

Sole owner?

Had Andres somehow bullied some judge into allowing a sale to go through despite Gary's attempts to stop them?

Had he bought Maxwell Mining to help me or, *and oh my God, I was going to puke,* was that all he'd been after since the beginning?

Prince of acquisitions.

That was his nickname at Volkov Industries.

But was I something he'd used to acquire his next big win?

My heart squeezed and immeasurable sadness filled me, like a rising tide I had no control over. I wanted to cry. But I didn't dare.

My eyes searched my husband's face, but he wasn't looking at me.

Handsome as sin, but colder than I'd ever seen him, Andres waved his hand in the air.

"Let's talk without the lawyers and the women,

yes?" Andres said, and Gary, the snake that he was, nodded.

"Go outside," Gary said, not even looking at his wife.

She flinched and pushed her chair back, the loud screech cut through the awkward silence, giving me time to address my husband.

The lawyers left one by one until only I remained.

"Andres," I hissed, staring at him with wide, terrified eyes.

What was he doing?

I thought we were there to protect Sammy.

I thought he cared.

I thought he was good.

I-I loved him.

Could I have been so wrong?

My head thudded as warring emotions raged battle inside me.

Hurt and anger.

Confusion and despair.

I didn't want to be dismissed. But I was clearly not wanted in that room. Andres spared me a single glance, and I wanted to tell him off. I wanted to slap his face.

But I stopped, frozen in his blue-gray gaze. I saw something there that quelled my rising hysteria.

Something that calmed the storm raging inside of me.

Emotion. Heat. Angst. Fury. And something else.

It was almost like a plea.

Like Andres was begging me to understand.

Whatever was brewing behind his suddenly cold eyes, I hoped I read him right. That silent entreaty moved me like nothing else could.

Trust me.

I could see the words like a neon sign burning between us.

Trust me.

He was asking me to put my faith in him. I'd already said I did.

I supposed it was time for me to prove it.

"Excuse me," I whispered, dipping my chin slightly before standing.

I exited the room after Gary's new wife and took a seat across the hall from her. She busied herself with her cell phone, and I tried not to freak out while I tried not to think about what was going on in there.

Mr. Orion excused himself to his office, and my lawyer nodded at me before taking his leave.

Odd.

I thought he'd stick around, but he didn't.

The minutes ticked by.

Three.

Seven.

I dropped my phone. Then picked it back up.

Ten.

Twelve.

Fuck.

What was taking so long?

I wasn't one hundred percent sure I understood my husband, but I knew he cared about Sammy. Even if he was only in this to get his hands on the company.

Mad or not about the high-handed way he'd dismissed me from the room, I believed Andres would do anything in his power to protect my son.

"You know he doesn't care about the kid, right?" Gary's wife spoke up.

"Excuse me?" I asked, stunned and a little wary.

"Your kid. Gary doesn't care about him. And he has no claim either."

"I'm sorry, I have no idea what you are talking about."

"Oh my God, are you this stupid? You guys went

to a fertility clinic, right?" she asked, enunciating slowly, like I was some idiot.

"Yeah. But how did you know about that?" I asked.

Yes, it was true, I did go to a fertility clinic. But it wasn't something I thought about a lot.

Gary had problems *performing* in bed with me. Like since day one. I was so damn green at the time, I believed it was my fault.

But we'd both wanted a child, or at least, *I'd* wanted a child. So yeah, I agreed to go to a reproductive specialist.

Gary had been adamant I kept that part of our journey to parenthood a secret.

He didn't want my father to think he wasn't man enough to impregnate his only daughter.

A fertility clinic had been the best answer to get the job done.

"You really are naïve, aren't you? Gary had a vasectomy when he was in his twenties. That kid is not his. He can't be," she said, rolling her eyes after dropping that bomb on me.

"What?" I gasped, horror pouring into me.

"He paid off the fertility doctor. Gary paid him off and made the man lie for him. Whoever your sperm donor was, it wasn't Gary. He only shoots blanks," she informed me.

Thunder roared inside my ears, and I was deaf, dumb, and blind to everything other than the bomb going off inside me.

Sammy wasn't Gary's son.

The truth was so damn obvious. He looked nothing like the man. Was nothing like him.

It all made sense.

Gary's coldness. His indifference.

He never cared about Sammy. Only pretended interest when my father was alive.

"W-why are you telling me this?" I asked, still holding on to a sliver of doubt.

If she was lying, I would kill her myself. This was too much. More than I hoped for.

It was everything.

"Because I told him! I told Gary if he tried hitting me the way he hit you, I would destroy him. He didn't believe me, but that's his problem. Excuse me, my ride is here," the future ex-Mrs. Peters said.

She stood up, her back ramrod straight, and she walked out of the waiting room.

I stood frozen for a solid thirty seconds before I raced back to the conference room and slammed the door open.

Andres looked cool and calm, sitting back while Gary raged about being cheated and about how miserable he was going to make our lives, *Sammy's life*, if Andres didn't give in.

I couldn't listen for another minute.

"Stop! STOP!" I shouted.

"Ellie, what is it?" Andres asked, leaning forward.

"His wife. She told m-me—"

"Shut up, you stupid fat bitch!" Gary shouted, losing his composure.

I never saw him look like that. Not even when he hit me.

"I fucking warned you," Andres growled.

Then I watched as my husband vaulted over the table, knocking Gary to the floor with one punch to the older man's jaw.

But Andres didn't stop there.

And because I had suddenly found a newfound thirst for violence where my ex was concerned, I closed the door.

Gary grunted. He begged. But Andres offered no quarter.

Eyes that I once thought wise and full of caring met mine, and I felt nothing.

Not even pity.

Which was why I did nothing to stop Andres

from straddling his chest and pummeling him in the face with his fist.

Over and over again, he hit him. And with every punch, I felt a piece of guilt, a piece of control that I wasn't even aware Gary still held over me, loosen its grip, and fly away into the ether.

With his fists, and his fury, Andres gave me something I didn't even know I was missing.

Andres gave me freedom.

I knew Ellie was pissed.

And it made me feel so fucking bad.

But I didn't have time to explain.

As soon as this was done, I would tell her everything. First, I needed to know if my intel was good.

"Look, Mr. Ramirez," Gary sneered like the condescending prick he was. "I know what you are. I looked you up. You work for those goddamn Russian gangsters. Now, I just wanna tell you, you didn't have to marry my ex to get her company."

"You mean my company. *I* own Maxwell Mining now."

"So you said, but you see, I am Maxwell Mining. I've been the managing VP for the last six years. I'll tell you what, you give me controlling interest. You let me run the company. And I'll let you raise my son," he said smugly.

"You would give me Sammy for a piece of Maxwell Mining?" I asked, not sure I could hate that smug motherfucker anymore than I already did.

"Sure. Hell, I can always fight that fat bitch in court. Tell the whole world how unfit she is to raise a child. Running out on her husband. Taking him from his father's loving arms. Letting him sleep in dirty shelters. What kind of mother does that? Oh, I will drag her through the mud," he said, a stupid grin on his face.

"Are you finished?" I asked, my control hanging on by a thread.

"Yes. I'm finished. That's my offer, now you think about it, Ramirez."

"First, if you ever talk about my wife again, I will rearrange your face. Second, I don't need to think about it," I said, inhaling deeply.

"Are you sure? You know, that kid is weak like his mother. When I get custody of him, and I will, I'm going to send him to boarding school. The meanest one I can find where the headmasters aren't afraid to use a little corporal punishment on sniveling brats like him."

"You fucking prick! When I said I didn't need to

think about it, I meant there was no contest between Sammy and some fucking company," I snapped, disgusted with this asshole.

I was one second away from beating the shit out of this motherfucker when the door flew open, and my wife barged in looking enraged and gorgeous.

My protective instincts were going crazy. I didn't want Gary to fucking look at her. I didn't want him breathing her air.

"Stop!" she shouted, her face red with rage.

"Ellie, what is it?"

"His wife. She told m-me—"

"Shut up, you stupid fat bitch!" Gary yelled at her.

And that was it. I snapped.

"I fucking warned you."

I jumped over the table separating us, and I unleashed hell on that motherfucker.

Thank fuck I did my homework on that law firm, right before I retained one of the partners as council, paying him a hefty six figures to do little more than keep my confidence.

I knew the room was soundproofed.

No one could hear Gary's whimpers and cries. That meant they also couldn't hear the pounding of my fists as they met his face or the sounds of skin and bones breaking.

Once he stopped moving, I stood up, spitting on the motherfucker.

He was still alive.

Barely.

I wasn't going to kill him with Ellie watching. But it was a close thing.

"Andres," she said my name like it gave her some relief to do so.

I stepped away from Gary, wiping my bloodied hands on the handkerchief I pulled from my pocket.

"You okay?" I asked.

"He's not Sammy's father," she said.

I frowned, not understanding her.

"What?"

"His new wife told me. See, Gary and I went to a fertility clinic, b-because he couldn't always perform. He said it was my fault. But she said he had a vasectomy years ago."

"What?" I repeated, my eyes wide.

"Gary paid off the doctor to impregnate me with donor sperm. He has no legal grounds to sue for visitation or custody. He's not Sammy's father," she repeated.

"Are you fucking serious?"

"Yes, Andres. I am so serious," she said, tears flowing from her eyes.

I cupped her cheek, pressing my forehead to hers. Relief filling me at hearing the truth.

"It doesn't matter who his sperm donor is, Sammy is *my son,* and you are *my wife,*" I said aloud, claiming them both.

"Yes. Yours," she nodded.

I knew she needed more, but I was still amped, and I couldn't speak gently like she deserved.

Not yet.

I grabbed my phone, calling the lawyer I'd retained, and my bodyguard to come into the room.

"Mr. Peters is sick. He had a seizure and hit his face. He needs a doctor," I said, ignoring the wide-eyed stare of my new attorney.

"Yes, sir, Mr. Ramirez," the lawyer said.

I turned my gaze to where Gary was dribbling blood onto the floor. Rage turned my vision red, but I would sit on that. Save it for another day.

"I'll be seeing you, Gary."

It was a promise.

"Take care of him. I'm taking my wife home."

The trip back to the condo was quiet, and I appreciated her giving me the silence I needed to calm down.

I was still fucking furious.

I'd wanted to kill Gary tonight.

But it was neither the time nor the place.

"Good evening, Mr. and Mrs. Ramirez. Just so you know, Sammy has been asleep for a while now," Nanny Rosa said when we walked into his bedroom to check on him.

"Thank you so much, Rosa," Ellie murmured, dropping a kiss on Sammy's head.

I followed suit, tucking him under the covers and brushing his soft hair back with my fingertips.

"The car is ready to drive you back. Unless you want to spend the night?" Ellie offered.

"Oh, I appreciate it, ma'am, but I'm good to go back. Thank you," the older woman said.

I dipped my chin and the bodyguard who'd accompanied us stepped forward to take Nanny Rosa's bag. He would walk the older woman to my car where another bodyguard and the driver waited. And they would make sure she returned to Adrik's place safe and sound.

"Want a nightcap?" I asked.

Ellie expelled a sigh and nodded, following me to the liquor cabinet. I grabbed two glasses and a bottle of Whiskey Neat, their new oak aged cherry label.

"Ice? Soda?"

"Both please."

I doctored hers and took mine straight, sliding her glass over to her side of the counter.

We took sips, and I waited, but my Ellie was as stubborn as I was, if not more.

God, I loved her.

"Ask me."

"Ask you what?" she replied.

"Ask me anything you want to know about tonight, or about anything at all, Wife. You ask, I tell. And vice versa."

She looked at me for a full beat, then nodded.

"Did you really buy Maxwell Mining?"

"I did," I said, watching her face fall. Then I continued.

"But I lied about being the owner."

"What? That makes no sense," she said, frowning.

I paused and decided I might as well just tell her the truth. Hell, I'd been so busy securing this deal, greasing hands to push it through.

It was a helluva thing getting a judge to rush a will through probate and to dismiss Gary's frivolous fucking suits.

I'd almost lost it a time or two, but I wasn't the *prince of acquisitions* for nothing.

Gary, that sleaze, was a moron. He didn't realize Maxwell Mining was sitting on several thousand acres of land, all right on top of rare earth mineral deposits. The kind that made princes of the paupers that were once the Volkov brothers.

I'd been working nonstop to make sure my wife and son got everything they had coming to them, so yeah, no more lies. It was time Ellie knew it all.

She was worth billions. The land, the money, the deals. It was all hers. And Sammy's.

There was more to it, though. Ellie wasn't just the owner of Maxwell Mining. She owned me.

Body, heart, and soul.

I belonged to that woman, and I wouldn't lie about it or hide. I wasn't ashamed of my feelings or of my devotion to her. And keeping secrets was far too costly.

"Okay," I began, backing her into our room.

"I'll tell you everything, but I need you to start stripping," I said.

Ellie's breath hitched, and she nodded, slipping her shoes off first. I groaned, loving the flash of skin as she lifted her pant legs and her ankles peeked out.

Now I knew why that was such a big thing a few centuries ago.

Ellie had Fanfuckingtastic ankles.

"Well? Are you going to start talking?" she asked, and I looked up, surprised.

My Lupina had grit. How could I forget?

"Right. So, first, I used my connections with Volkov Industries to push the sale of Maxwell Mining through despite certain restrictions pending investigation," I said, stepping out of my own shoes.

I raised my eyebrows, and Ellie unsnapped her pants, pulling her sweater over her head. She paused, and I grinned wider.

"I had those cleared, by the way. Your inheritance, everything from your father's estate, should all revert to you by the end of business tomorrow. As for the company," I said, mulling over my words.

Ellie took my pause as something else, and I was not complaining as she pushed her pants down her hips, allowing them to fall.

Standing there in a black lace bra and panties, my wife looked like a fucking seductress.

My cock strained inside my pants, thumping against the zipper, and I groaned, pulling off my shirt and undoing my buckle.

"Andres?" she prompted, and I noticed she looked a little nervous.

"There's no nice way to say this, but your father really fucked you when it came to the company, Angel. He absolutely did not want you to have it, and he worded it in such a way that I couldn't give you ownership if I tried. So, what I did was, I gave it to Sammy. But since you're his mother, and legal guardian, it is yours until he comes of age."

"What?"

"Sammy owns Maxell Mining," I repeated.

"I don't understand. So, you didn't do all this just for the company," she whispered, her pouty lips opening.

"What? No. Of course not. Sammy is the sole owner and heir of Maxwell Mining and all its holdings with you as his mother and legal guardian, you can use his vote however you want. I never wanted Maxwell Mining, Ellie. But I hope you won't mind, but I already started looking into ways to improve the company."

"You never wanted it?"

"No. It's not mine. But I can help make it better for you, for Sammy, when he gets older. If you let me. It's kind of what I do for Volkov Industries. What kind of father would I be if I didn't look out for my son's future?"

"And you did all this before you even knew he wasn't Gary's?" she asked, and I could see her surprise.

"Lupina, all I ever needed to know in order for

me to love Sammy like he's my own child is to know he's yours."

I watched her connect the dots, saw the exact moments when she understood what I was trying to say, and it was like the light at the end of a long, cold, dark tunnel.

Ellie walked into my space, placing her hands on my shoulders. She leaned back so she could look at my face, and I loved that she was so much smaller than me.

So much softer than I was.

So much warmer.

Kinder.

Better.

Ellie was good.

So damn good.

It made me feel protective, possessive, and so damn lucky to have her.

"Are you trying to say you married me because you love me, Husband?"

I placed my hands on her waist and dragged her closer, not stopping until I felt the hard points of her breasts pressed against my chest through the skimpy piece of lace covering her.

"Yeah, Wife, that's what I'm saying."

I nuzzled her nose with mine, breathing her

breath, and just held onto her. I was trying to give her the space and time she needed to come to terms with our new reality.

"This was never a marriage of convenience. I didn't wed you out of pity or greed," I growled, then thought about it a second. "Well, maybe greed. But not the kind of greed you think."

I didn't need Maxwell Mining or what would add up to over a billion dollars of personal wealth for her and her son once I finished going through their assets and increasing their holdings.

I had my own money. My own job. My own properties.

But I would never leave what was theirs to rot. And I would certainly never leave it in the hands of lesser men like Gary fucking Peters.

"What do you mean, then?" she whispered.

"I didn't marry you for your father's company or your inheritance, Ellie. I married you because I can't fucking live without you. I'm greedy for you, Angel, only you," I confessed, and it felt so goddamn good.

It was like a weight had been lifted off my chest. A veil had been torn from my eyes, and I could finally see what was right in front of me.

Her. Only her.

Ellie sighed, lifting herself up onto her tippy toes.

She crushed my mouth with hers, and I moaned when I felt her tongue slide in.

"Get on the bed, Husband," she commanded.

I couldn't even form words to tell her I would.

Instead, I just picked her up, cupping my hands on her ass and trying not to stumble when she wrapped her legs around my waist and pressed her hot core to my front.

"Fuck," I growled, barely making it across the bedroom floor.

Both of us were panting, moaning, desperate for more. I kicked off my pants, stepping out of them without missing a beat.

This frenzied collision of need and want was like nothing I ever felt.

I was beyond attracted. I was fucking obsessed. Wildly, completely, and irrevocably committed to this woman.

"What do you need, Angel?"

"You," she said, licking into my mouth and tugging my bottom lip with her teeth.

I groaned as Ellie moved to her knees on the mattress. I was still standing, so she was at just the right height to tug my briefs down my thighs.

"Andres, I need it," Ellie whimpered.

I growled and reached behind her, unhooking her bra and pulling it off her perfect tits.

Kneeling on the bed in just her panties, her cheeks flushed and her hazel eyes half-closed with desire. Ellie closed her hand around my cock, her lips parted on a gasp and I fucking ached for her.

She looked like a wet dream come to life.

Fuck.

"Goddamn. Let me taste those tits, Angel. Fuck. Give 'em here," I growled.

I lifted her breasts in my hands, testing their weight and loving the feel of them. They were the perfect size. Her pink puckered nipples were just begging me to taste them.

Groaning, I bent my head and sucked one, then the other, into my mouth. Ellie moaned my name, tugging on my hair.

So fucking good.

"Please," she begged.

I pulled back, allowing her sweet cherry-tipped nipple to pop free from the warm suction of my mouth.

"You want more, Wife? Tell me."

"I want more, Andres. Please."

I placed my hand in the center of her chest and pushed her back onto the bed. Her knees were still bent, and I slid them out from under her until they were straight, rubbing my hand over her covered mound, her hips, her thighs, her calves.

Every inch of this woman was made for me.

She was something to worship.

Something to covet and cherish.

But she was also a she-wolf. Fierce and wild.

But sometimes, even an alpha like my woman needed her man to take charge.

"Should I eat you out first, Wife? Lick this sweet cunt until you come on my mouth? Or should I fill you with my dick, take you hard and rough? Tell me."

"Andres," she whined.

"What is it, Lupina? Are you wet? Did you ruin your panties? I better take them off and check," I growled.

I grabbed the material from the sides and yanked them down as far as I could, her splayed legs making it impossible to take them all the way off. Pulling on the tiny little bit of elastic, I ripped her panties off.

I pushed her knees down, exposing her glistening slit to my hungry gaze.

"Fuck, Angel. You're soaked."

I bent my head, swiping my tongue along her seam.

"Fuck. You're so good," I groaned, closing my mouth over her clit.

"Andres, I need you," she said, pulling my hair, lifting herself up on her elbows.

I raised my head, her arousal dripping from my lips.

Goddamn.

Her hair was wild. The short curls in gorgeous disarray. Her skin was flushed, her nipples hard, and her breasts bouncing with every inhale.

Legs still splayed, I had the perfect view of her pussy, so pink and wet and ready for me.

She looked like a goddess.

She looked like mine.

"Husband, I need you to fill me with your cock, please," she said, and how was I supposed to resist that?

Ellie's big, warm hazel eyes met mine, and the look on her face matched how I felt inside. With a growl, I climbed up her body, notching my dick at her slick entrance.

I ran my fingers through her hair, pulling on the strands and moving her where I wanted her. Then I fused my mouth to hers, sucking her tongue, marking her as mine.

It was boorish, caveman behavior, but I couldn't help it.

I needed to claim her.

To brand her.

I needed to have all of Ellie. Wanted to stamp myself all over her now that she knew I loved her.

Now that I'd confessed my feelings.

"You're mine, aren't you, Angel? You're mine. You belong to me. Tell me," I growled, sliding in an inch.

"Please," she whined, clawing at my back, and I withdrew.

"Andres," she begged.

"Tell me," I repeated.

"Yours, I'm yours."

"Good Girl," I grunted, pushing in two inches, then pausing.

Fuck.

Her tight channel squeezed me.

"Your home is with me. I'll always take care of you. You believe me, Angel? Tell me."

I pressed in some more. Ellie gasped and her pussy squeezed me even tighter as I flexed my hips, out then in, sliding deeper with each stroke.

"My home is with you," she said and moaned, arching her back.

"Always with me. Only me," I grunted and slammed my hips against hers.

"Only you. You'll always take care of me," she said, clawing at my hips.

"Tell me you'll never leave me. Say you belong to me."

"I will never leave you, Andres, because I belong to you and because you love me," she replied, tears rolling down her face.

Ellie pulled me down to her, but she didn't kiss me like I expected. She looked into my eyes first, her mouth open as I stroked inside her so fucking deep, and I knew she was close to coming.

"You love me, Andres."

"I love you, Ellie," I said, worshipping her with words, with my stare, with my body.

I withdrew, then stroked slowly back in, changing the tempo, raising the heat. I was so ready to explode, but the tenderness I felt had me reeling. I bent to kiss her, but she pulled back and I frowned.

"Ellie—"

"You love me," she whispered, touching my face and wrapping her legs around my waist. "And I love you. So much. Ever since I met you."

My mind went blank, and thunder roared inside my veins.

"Say it again."

"I love you, Andres," she repeated.

I froze for a moment, maybe two.

Then I moved.

Joy filled my veins, passion fueled my fire, and I slammed my hips, pounding into my wife's sweet pussy.

Our moans reverberated inside the bedroom, and I was grateful I'd spent the extra money getting it soundproofed.

My Lupina was a noisy little thing.

She was so fucking perfect.

I rutted into her, pistoning my hips, knowing her pussy could take all the fervor and pent up passion I'd been building up for her.

Christ.

Fuck.

I'd been sitting on my feelings for more than half a year.

I wasn't gentle. I couldn't be.

I never knew I could feel this way. Never expected her claim on me to have such an effect.

This wasn't what the movies told you sex would be like after the first time you said *I love you.*

This was rough.

Wild.

Hot.
Messy.
Desperate.
Joyful.
And needy.
It was so fucking raw. And it was good.
Really good.
Ellie was just as in it as I was. Her eyes sparkled with intensity. Her warm, soft skin surrounded me.

I felt her everywhere. Her arms were around me, her legs held on, her hips lifted to meet mine, and her sex spasmed around my thick cock as I pumped into her repeatedly.

She was everywhere. My everything. Filling every inch of my mind, my body, my heart, and my soul.

"I love you, Wife. Now show me how much you love me and come all over my cock."

"Love you so much, Husband," she cried out, her pussy spasming around me.

Every flutter and quiver of her needy little cunt sent me farther over the edge. I grabbed her hips, my fingers bruising, and I lifted her, switching our positions.

Ellie was still lost in her orgasm, and I was desperate to chase her there. I lifted her by her sweet ass, fucking her on my cock, and grinding her slippery little clit onto my pubis.

"Again, Wife. Come again," I commanded.

"I-I can't," she cried.

But that was a lie. I knew she could.

Her hot pussy felt so good, I was close, too. But first, I was going to make sure she got there again.

"Now, Angel. Be my Good Wife and come for me. Right fucking now," I growled, sucking her nipple into my mouth, and biting down while I flexed my hips and pulled her tight to me.

Her cunt contracted, and she moaned, long and loud. Then I exploded inside of her, painting her walls with my cum.

Blind, deaf, and dumb to everything except the sensation of having my wife cling to me in the sweaty, sticky aftermath of what was the most phenomenal sex I'd ever had, I sucked in air, trying to catch my breath.

When I first saw Ellie, I knew I wanted her.

The attraction I'd felt towards the woman was off the charts. But I didn't know I would become so addicted to her, so damn crazy that I was borderline psychotic where she was concerned.

The lines I crossed were pretty big. Stalking, interfering, inserting myself into her life.

I was unhinged where Ellie was concerned.

But the good news was, she was into me, too.

My wife was all I ever wanted. Finding out she wanted me as well was a bonus. But wanting wasn't enough.

Tonight, Ellie gave me what I really needed. What I'd craved all along. Tonight was all about possession.

Love and possession might sound like different things. I mean, I heard the saying *love someone, set them free*.

I would do anything for Ellie. But I was keeping her. I was never letting go.

I wasn't an abusive asshole, though. I preferred to think the kind of freedom that saying meant was the freedom to live her life and be who she was, not freedom from me.

That I could do. Ellie had my total and complete support.

She had my loyalty. My devotion.

I hugged her tighter, sliding off the bed and standing to my full height with my sated wife in my arms.

"Where are we going?" she whispered, still coming down from the high of coming apart twice in my arms.

"Shower," I said, kissing her temple.

We both needed a shower, and then I'd take her back to bed and hold her for the rest of the night.

For the rest of my life.

Satisfaction hummed through my body, buzzed in my veins. Contentment filled me as I turned the water on, making sure the temperature was right before stepping into the enormous shower with Ellie still wrapped around me.

"Stand," I whispered, and she did.

Or, well, she tried. I kept my arm around her back, steadying her as she regained her balance. We washed in comfortable silence and my gaze roamed over every inch of her with a newfound proprietorship.

She was mine. Completely mine.

For the first time, Ellie had given herself to me, knowing the truth in my heart. The way I felt. My need to possess her. Even better, she had claimed me right back.

And I'd never been so fucking happy.

He loves me.

And I love him.

The night after the meeting with the lawyers was the first night Andres stayed in our bed until morning.

Waking up with his thick dick pressed against my hip had my mouth watering, and giving my husband a blow job was the perfect way to express myself.

Andres reciprocated. Twice.

And for the first time in my adult life, I knew what it felt like to be loved and to be in love.

Really in love.

And it was better than I imagined.

Things had slowly changed since the night I confessed my feelings to Ellie.

It felt like we were more of a union now. More a family.

Pride burned in my eyes as I pictured them before I left for work that morning.

Ellie was wearing a pair of stretchy jeans and a fuzzy gray sweater, and Sammy was getting ready to visit the preschool we were looking to send him to starting that January since he missed the fall semester.

Ellie and I had spent a few days researching programs we felt would be good for him, and today was the first interview.

I was meeting them there at ten o'clock, but I had to handle some things first at work.

My phone buzzed, and I looked down, frowning when I saw the contact.

It was a message from the Sigma International bodyguard I'd enlisted to tail Gary Peters after our little meeting.

The motherfucker had given him the slip.

Fuck.

"Morning, cousin," Marat said, walking into my office.

"Morning," I replied, eyeing him warily.

Still known as the face of Volkov Industries, Marat was more than met the eye. Something his enemies had to learn firsthand.

Luckily, I was not one of them.

But I had no time for reunions or whatever Marat wanted to chat about.

I needed to get someone out looking for Gary. With Ellie and Sammy out and about today, even with a driver and bodyguard, I was on fucking edge as it was.

Knowing Gary was on the run was not a comfort in any way shape or form. I needed to call Ellie.

"What's up?" I asked Marat, hoping to shoo him along so I could phone my wife.

"Nothing. Just thought I could spend some time bonding with my favorite cousin."

"You only learned I was your cousin a few weeks ago. How can I be your favorite?" I asked blandly.

"Probably because I don't know of any others," he replied with a shrug.

"Idiot," a gruff voice said from the doorway and we both turned to see Adrik standing there. "Get in my office, both of you."

I followed Marat and Adrik to his office, wondering what was going on. Josef was already inside, and he didn't look so happy.

"What's going on?" I asked.

"Anything you want to tell us, *cousin*? Like how you confronted your wife's ex-husband in a law firm we don't own and proceeded to beat the man to a pulp in front of witnesses?" Adrik snapped.

Eyebrows raised, I looked from one man to the other, stopping with Josef when he lifted his phone to show me a picture of a beaten and bloody Gary Peters.

I heaved a sigh.

"What? It's not like you haven't done anything like that before," I grumbled, rubbing the back of my neck with my hand.

"Why wouldn't you come to us for help with this?" Adrik spat, slamming his hands on the desk.

"Ellie's ex-husband is my problem to deal with," I said, shaking my head.

"That is where we beg to differ, cuz. You see, we're family. That makes this asshole all of our problems," Marat replied.

Emotion started to build inside of me. I never had this. Family, camaraderie, or whatever it was.

It was new.

It was different.

And it felt good.

"Tell us everything you know about him," Adrik instructed, and I took a seat.

"He's an abusive fucking blight on humanity," I growled. "He hit her. He threatened Sammy. He's tried to weasel his way into positions of power within her father's company. Thought he was going to get the whole shebang once the old man died. But he didn't. And the fucker took it out on her," I said, barely able to contain my fury.

"Fuck," Adrik spat.

"You didn't kill him?" Marat questioned.

"I was keeping him alive because I thought he was Sammy's father and I couldn't do that to the boy," I growled.

"What do you mean you thought he was Sammy's father?" Adrik asked.

"Oh, well, this motherfucking prince tricked Ellie, berated her into thinking she was at fault for his limp fucking dick. They used a fertility doctor, and good ol' Gary bribed the fucking guy to knock her up with donor sperm."

Just saying it out loud brought a wave of rage flowing through me, I didn't realize I'd been sitting on.

I was going to find out who that fucking doctor was. And I was going to kill him myself.

What he did was unethical, immoral, and a gross violation of my wife.

Even if she wasn't married to me at the time, Ellie was mine.

"Josef?" I growled, and the man nodded, reading my mind.

"On it," he said, shooting off a text.

"So, you had a meeting with this *man*? For what purpose?" Adrik asked.

"He threatened to sue for visitation," I began, and then proceeded to explain everything that had happened up to me beating the shit out of Gary Peters.

"Again, cousin, I must ask, why not kill him?"

I sighed.

Might as well tell them the truth. If anyone understood my compulsion to do right by Ellie, it was these three men.

"Because I didn't want her to see that. Didn't want her to know I was capable of that kind of violence," I confessed.

"Understandable, and fucked up," Marat said, slapping a hand on my back.

I rubbed my own hand over my face. Too many fucking emotions were batting at me to do more than that.

"Look, I know I dropped a bomb on you at the wedding. It doesn't have to change how you treat me, though," I said, and they all scoffed.

"Are you fucking kidding? Bro, you're family," Marat said, as if that explained it all.

"We take care of family, blood or otherwise," Adrik added.

"Not to mention the fact that our wives have all bonded, forming a friendship that means a lot to each one of them. Knowing her friend was close to this piece of shit sent Merdith into a frenzy," Josef said, adding his two cents.

"Fuck. I'm sorry, I didn't think it was something I needed to trouble you all with. I love my wife. I've loved her for a while. As for Sammy, he's mine. They both are. And I protect what's mine," I said, and it felt really fucking good to share this with them.

"Then we will, too. Because, Andres, you are our family. You and yours are also *ours*. You are Volkov," Andres growled, his Russian accent he'd almost gotten rid of peeking out at the last.

"Thank you," I replied, holding his intense gaze for a beat.

"You got him pretty good," Marat mumbled, looking at the photo that Josef had apparently sent to each of them.

"Broke his jaw, shattered his cheekbone, and destroyed his nose," Adrik murmured.

"Yeah, I dabbled in MMA when I was in college," I replied.

"Really?"

"Yeah. I mean, I can shoot and use a knife okay, but I prefer using my hands."

"I get it," Adrik said. "We should spar sometime."

"No thanks. I mean, I'm good, but you're a fucking beast, Adrik."

"Ha! I suppose I am," he said with a smirk.

"You know, Andres, we've done many bad things, but we've worked hard to become a legitimate business. Even harder to bury our not so clean past. But we still have connections," Adrik said, his voice even.

I nodded.

What could I say?

I knew all about that chapter in the Volkov family dedicated to criminal undertakings. And really, I was fine with it.

Maybe that made me a worse man than I thought I was, but I didn't have it in me to judge them.

Truth was there wasn't that much difference between the corporate world and the criminal one. Though, perhaps one was more honest than the other.

Of course, it was up to interpretation which was which.

"It all comes down to fundamentals, but in my experience, every powerful organization steps over the line now and then," Josef stated.

"Yes. Agreed. I suppose it is up to Karma to bring us all to task eventually," Adrik replied.

"You know how karma deals with men like us?" Marat asked, a grin splitting his stupid handsome face.

"How?" I asked.

"It gives us daughters."

I'd expected someone to laugh, but instead, all four of us went quiet.

My brain short-circuited. Thoughts going immediately to Ellie.

I imagined the others were thinking of the women in their lives.

Marat would undoubtedly picture Destiny and Lucy. While visions of Michaela and Sofia filled Adrik's head. Meredith, with her swollen abdomen, was likely consuming Josef's every thought.

I couldn't blame them for pausing. I couldn't blame myself either for the sudden intense joy that raged through me at the thought of having a daughter, of adding to my beautiful family.

A son.

A daughter.

A life.

With Ellie. My Lupina.

I was really looking forward to that.

Picturing her swollen with our baby was enough to make me cry. The woman had me on my knees.

Did she know?

How could she not?

I should have felt vulnerable. Maybe some thought me weak. But all I could feel was pride. Pride that she was mine, and that I was hers.

Christ, I loved her.

"Okay, well, I hate to break up this reunion, but after that prick was seen by one of our doctors, he took off. My man tried to track him, but he gave him the slip," Josef said, and I exhaled.

"Shit. Yeah, he texted me too, before I came in here," I said, reaching for my cell. "Fuck. I forgot to text Ellie."

I dialed her number and frowned as the line went straight to voicemail.

"What the fuck? She's not answering," I growled, fear causing the vein in my neck to throb.

"Is she using a Sigma driver today?" Josef asked.

I nodded, tracking her phone.

"Her phone is stopped at the Safari Playground. It's on 91st Street off Central Park West," I shouted as I took off for the elevator.

Adrik, Marat, and Josef were right on my heels, and I froze after I hit the button for the elevator. It was a private one. Faster than the general car.

But it was still going to take a second, and during that time, I met their determined gazes one at a time.

There was no point telling them they didn't have to come with me. They would, anyway.

Just like I would be there if they ever needed my support.

Because Adrik was right.

I am a Volkov.

I am family.

My wife and son are family.

That meant Ellie and Sammy were theirs to protect, too.

"If Gary is there. If that prick is threatening them, I'll end him this time," I said.

"Got it. Our boys will meet us," Marat replied, rolling his shoulders.

The elevator pinged, and the doors opened. We got on, silent, lethal, all of us on the same page.

My mind wandered, and it occurred to me this might be the first time four alpha wolves headed to Central Park for a common purpose.

To protect theirs.

When I met Ellie, I became immediately obsessed with her. The attraction I felt?

Hell.

That wasn't even the right word anymore. Whatever it was, it defied nature. Laughed in the face of Newton's law of universal gravitation.

We stalked over to the two SUVs Josef had waiting for us and we split up. Me with Adrik, and Josef and Marat in the second one.

"We will find her," Adrik said.

I nodded. We had to. There was no other choice.

But even as I held on to my fear for my own sanity's sake, I thought of my beautiful wife.

She looked so innocent, but beneath that soft exterior, Ellie was a fucking wolf.

My Lupina.

People lied.

Everyone did.

At one time or other, every single human being on the face of the planet has told a fib or a lie.

But my Ellie? She lied without ever meaning to.

Her whole appearance was a lie.

She made you think she was this shy, timid, scared little thing. This soft, fragile, sheltered carbon copy of a woman. But nothing could be further from the truth.

Ellie wasn't some burned out version of herself.

Ellie was the fire.

She was iron.

She was steel

She was mine

All fucking mine.

And if Gary Peters laid one finger on her, he was going to find out the hard way what that meant.

Life was perfect. I never thought it could be. But suddenly, it was.

Andres loves me.

He loves Sammy.

We're building a life together.

I had a basket of sourdough proofing on the countertop. I was going to make that rosemary focaccia Andres loved so much with dinner tonight. Steak and asparagus in a hollandaise sauce.

For Sammy, I was making another side dish, his favorite homemade mac and cheese. He'd already told me the macaroni monster in his tummy was hungry for it.

"Sammy!" I called my son's name, frowning.

He'd already been warned we had fifteen minutes to spare at the park. No more than that.

I didn't want to be late for our appointment at the preschool we were looking at for Sammy. It had great reviews and a long waitlist. But luckily, we were able to snag an interview.

I walked past a group of hippopotamuses at the Safari Playground, some of them half sunk into the soft rubbery ground that was safe for toddlers and preschool aged children to play on.

I knew we shouldn't have stopped, but we were too early for our appointment to visit the preschool we were considering. Plus, it was a bright and sunny November morning, perfect for some outdoor fun.

"Sammy?!" I called again, ducking around a tall tree to check behind the slide.

In the summer, there would be sprinklers in that park, bathing the children with cold water from tiny little spouts on the hippos. I couldn't wait for Sammy to see it then, but right now, I needed to find him.

There were only a handful of people there, and I became more and more frantic as the seconds ticked by. I only glanced at my phone for one second to check the time, but it must have been long enough for Sammy to wander.

Shit.

Fuck.

I was a bad mother.

No.

I shook my head. That was ridiculous. I was not a bad mother. I loved my son, and I took good care of him. He probably just got distracted by some squirrels or something.

My heart tightened. I couldn't breathe. I was starting to panic.

Where was he?

It felt like my soul was about to shatter.

I wanted to scream. To rant. To rave. I wanted Andres.

He would help.

He would find Sammy.

"Sammy? SAMMY!" I screamed, ignoring the pitying glances of strangers as I raced from one bench to the other.

"Hey, are you okay?"

"My son! I-I can't find my son," I whimpered.

I tripped over my own two feet, landing hard on my knees, and tearing my pants. I bit back my tears and pushed myself off the ground.

"Mrs. Ramirez! This way," Eduardo, the man

Andres assigned to be our bodyguard, called my name, just as he took off down a path.

My heart stuttered inside my chest. If the bodyguard was running that meant one thing.

Someone took Sammy.

Someone bigger than him.

Someone who could hurt him.

No. No. No!

A scream tore from my throat, and I started to run as fast as my short, chubby legs could carry me.

People passed by in a blur, but I kept my sight zeroed in on the bodyguard who was pounding the pavement, gun raised and pointed at a man holding my son.

He'd stopped behind one of those smaller brick buildings that were scattered across the park for whatever reason. I whipped my head from side to side, but no one was around.

Arms wide, I tried to approach the dirty man holding my boy.

"Stop! Drop your gun or the boy dies!" a familiar voice snapped.

I squinted my eyes.

Could that be? Oh my God!

It was Gary. But not the Gary I knew.

"Do as he says," I told Eduardo, stepping in front of him with my hands raised.

"Ma-am," Eduardo began, but I shook my head.

"Nothing matters except Sammy, understand," I said through my clenched jaw.

"Mommy," Sammy whimpered, and he had tears in his little eyes.

It had started as a nice day, but suddenly the sky was gray and overcast. There was a bite in the air. A frigidity I equated with fear.

My entire body trembled with rage, but I stepped forward, my gaze never wavering from my tiny, trusting son.

"It's okay, Sweetie. Mommy's here."

"Mommy, he said he has Rocky and that he's sick," Sammy whined.

"It'll be okay, Baby. Rocky is just fine," I told my boy, angry at Gary, furious that he somehow found out about my son's pet.

"Just give Sammy to me," I said the last to Gary.

"This wasn't how it was supposed to go," my ex tried to speak, but it was difficult to understand him.

Dark dribble leaked from the corner of his mouth. His face was distorted, badly bruised, and swollen from where Andres had beaten him.

He looked terrible. But it wasn't enough.

I wished he'd killed him. This version of Gary was completely unrecognizable from the man I knew. But maybe it was more like him than his regular appearance let on.

It was good he looked like a stranger. Maybe Sammy didn't recognize him either with that crooked, swollen nose, two blackened eyes, and his broken jaw.

"Get over here! You're coming with me. Do it, and I'll let this little bastard go," Gary said, his eyes crazed.

I nodded, eager to get my son to safety and more than willing to trade places with him.

"Mrs. Ramirez, I can't let you—" Eduardo started, but I shook my head, warning him to be silent.

"It's fine. It's okay. I'll go with you, just let him go. Let Sammy go."

"Mommy? I want Rocky. I want Dad," Sammy cried, and my heart broke for my son.

"You're okay, Baby. Rocky is okay, too," I told him.

"Dad?" scoffed Gary, but I ignored him.

"Dad is going to come get you and bring you home. Mommy will be okay," I spoke directly to Sammy, knowingly lying to him for the first time since I left Gary.

I took one step, then another. Moving closer to Gary in an effort to keep his attention on me.

Sammy was full-on wailing. I thought it would bring some attention to us, but I should have known better.

We were in Central Park. The largest recreation center on the whole island of Manhattan. Arguably the most famous park on the East Coast.

There were thousands of visitors daily. More than that. But no one heard his cries. Or if they did, they thought nothing of it.

No one noticed the drama ensuing right there in broad daylight. No one came around the building to ask questions. And no one got involved because we were in the City, and people minded their own business in the city.

Life was hard, sure, but so what? Everyone had their baggage. One crying kid wasn't noteworthy. One ex couple having a spat wasn't the end of the world.

But to me, this could be. And I wasn't going to let anything happen to my baby boy.

"Shut up, you brat," Gary sniveled and dropped Sammy on the hard ground.

"No!" I yelled.

The gun in Gary's hand was too close to Sammy's

head. I made a run at the same time someone behind me roared. Gary jerked his hand up, he had his leg lifted as if to kick Sammy.

I couldn't let him do that. I ran harder. Time seemingly frozen until I reached him.

A sound I didn't recognize spilled from my lips as I used all my strength to tackle Gary to the ground, grabbing the hand holding the gun.

Out of the corner of my eye, I saw someone grab Sammy off the floor. I prayed my boy was safe as I tore the gun from Gary's hands and spun it around, aiming for his face.

Then I squeezed the trigger.

We pulled up to the playground just as I caught sight of Ellie running. I jumped out of the car, chasing after my wife.

I yelled. I know I did. But she didn't or couldn't hear me.

Fear like I'd never known pumped through my veins.

When I rounded the squat brick building and saw Gary with a gun aimed at my son. All rationale left my brain.

Pure, undiluted fury moved faster than lightning, louder than thunder, consuming me until I was a living, breathing personification of vengeance.

Ellie charged at Gary, and that piece of shit dropped Sammy onto the ground.

I ran.

I wasn't going to get there in time.

Fuck.

I flicked my gaze at Ellie, knowing what she would want, and wishing like fuck I could tear myself in two.

I reached Sammy first.

"You're okay," I said as I clutched him to my chest.

Adrik, Marat, and Josef were right behind me, and I looked up to find the latter sliding to a stop beside me just as a gunshot rang out.

I handed Sammy to Josef and spun around, my heart in my fucking throat.

"ELLIE!" I roared, dropping to my knees, and grabbing the gun from her hand.

"Andres? Oh, my God! Andres? Sammy?"

I pulled her into my embrace, running my hands over her body to check for injury.

"Are you okay? Angel, are you hurt?" I asked, my voice breaking.

Someone had called the police. I heard the sirens in the background, But I didn't give two shits.

"I'm fine. I'm okay. You came. You're here.

Sammy?" Ellie whimpered, uncontrolled tears streaming down her face.

"He's fine. Josef!" I yelled.

"Mommy! Daddy!" Sammy's frightened voice reached my ears, and I opened my arms for Josef to hand us our son.

"I thought I was too late. I'm so sorry. So sorry," I said, biting back my own tears.

Clinging to my wife and son, I picked Ellie up, princess-style, while she held onto Sammy. I walked past the barricade the cops had set up, Adrik and Marat were dealing with them.

I trusted them to get through all the politics of what had just happened. It was nothing they hadn't done before.

But I couldn't think about that. I didn't have the headspace.

Fuck, I almost lost them.

I climbed into the SUV, sliding Ellie into a seat so she could put Sammy beside her. I carefully buckled them both in and told the driver to go straight to our condo.

"Is he okay?" I asked a half an hour later after Ellie finally emerged from Sammy's room.

Her eyes were puffy and her face blotchy from crying. She had rips in her pants, and a small bruise on her cheek where she must have gotten hit when she collided with Gary.

"Yeah, he's sleeping, and Rocky is curled up at his feet," she said, walking over to where I stood, a tumbler of whiskey in my hand.

She took it from me and knocked it back, hissing at the powerful stuff. I was sure it burned going down, but I didn't fault her for drinking it. It was my third one already, and my hands were still shaking.

"Ellie, I am so sorry—"

"Sammy didn't recognize Gary," she blurted, wringing her hands, looking everywhere but not at me.

"No?" I asked.

It was clear she was having some feelings about what happened, and I needed to let her have them.

But I was nervous as fuck. Scared, she wanted to leave me.

Goddamn.

I would do anything she asked if I could just keep her.

Please, Ellie.

"He, uh, just thinks it was a strange man who tried to hurt him. I'm going to call the therapist tomorrow and get her advice, but I think it's better that he think it was a stranger until he's much older. What do you think?"

My heart stuttered.

If she was asking me what I thought, she had to be staying, right?

You didn't ask someone a question like that if you didn't care.

"Andres?"

"Ellie," I started.

But because I couldn't stand to be so close and not touching her, I cupped my hand around the back of her neck and pulled her to me.

"Anything you want to tell Sammy is fine with me, Ellie. Just tell me this means you're staying. You're not leaving me," I said.

"Andres," she whimpered, and shoved against my chest. But I tightened my hold.

"Please don't push me away, Angel. I can't stand it. I can't bear it. I'm so sorry. I fucked up. I failed. I didn't protect you," I said, blubbering all over her and myself and making a fool out of me.

"Andres," she said more forcefully, and fuck, I couldn't go against her wishes. I released her.

But she didn't pull away. Instead, she cupped my cheeks in her hand and pressed her mouth to mine.

"What?" I whispered.

"You crazy man. I love you. I'm not going anywhere. I thought maybe, maybe you would think I was tainted because I killed a man—"

"Stop right there," I said.

Pulling her closer, I leaned down, kissing her just because I could. Because she let me. And because I needed to.

"I love you. I would never think badly of you," I told her honestly. "But you're wrong, Ellie. You didn't kill a man. Gary was living on borrowed time. His days were already numbered. Understand?"

"Yes, Andres," she said, and a small smile tilted the corner of her lips.

"That's it, Angel. Smile for me," I said, kissing her again. "I need that smile. Need your joy. Your light. Fuck Ellie, I love you so much. Swear you will never leave me."

"Never. I will never leave you. I need you too, Andres."

Walking my wife backwards to the couch, I reversed our positions, so that she was standing in front of me, and I was sitting on the couch.

Outside, the storm clouds gathered around, shrouding Manhattan in a glittery sort of blackness. Then, suddenly, lightning cracked across the sky and thunder boomed. Thanksgiving was in two days, but instead of snow, we had wind and rain.

Typical weather. But I didn't give a shit about the rain.

Only that it pitched the room into darkness, and I loved Ellie in black.

I licked my lips, watching the rise and fall of her chest.

"Show me how much you need me, Ellie. Let me see you, Lupina." I growled.

Her eyes widened, and I knew her first instinct was to object. I undid the buttons of my shirt, pealed at the way her eyes danced over my skin as I revealed my body to her inch by inch.

Next was my buckle. I unfastened my pants, tugging them down my hips, and bringing my boxers with them.

Dick in hand, I watched my wife's eyes widen. She licked her lips as I squeezed my balls and stroked my shaft.

"Take off your clothes and sit on my cock like a Good Wife."

oly. Fuck

I licked my lips. Desire warred with misgivings. But I'd just been through a lot and I needed something to make me feel grounded, anchored, part of the real world again.

I wasn't a sex goddess.

I didn't think I was good at this kind of thing.

But I wanted to be. And for Andres, I would try.

He loved me. He wouldn't judge me or make fun of me. And as I quickly stripped, too eager to feel him inside me to even attempt to go slow, he watched.

Andres' eyes never left my body as I pulled off my clothes until I was standing there in my plain black cotton thong.

"Leave those on," he said, and I nodded.

I expected him to tug my hand or drag me down on top of him, but Andres didn't move.

Biting my lip, I took the first step. I sat on his lap. Pressing my hands to his shoulders, I leaned down and took his mouth.

He tasted so good. Like whiskey and lemons. I licked into his mouth deeper, moaning as I rubbed my nipples against his hair-roughened chest.

My hips flexed, my cotton-covered slit rubbing against him. He was so hard. His cock pulsed against me as his hands grabbed my ass, grinding me down.

"Fuck, Lupina, your pussy is so hot. It's searing me through these panties," he said.

"Andres, need you," I whimpered.

"Move them to the side, Angel. Let me feel how much you need me," he groaned.

I reached between us and moved my panties, moaning when his fat head bumped against my hand. I guided him to my dripping entrance, pressing down when he made no move to do it for me.

"That's it, angel. Take me. Take my cock into your body," he groaned, and I did.

I fucking did. I lowered my hips until every inch of his delicious dick was inside me.

"Andres?"

"Ride me, Angel. Show me what you like. Use my body to get yourself off. I wanna feel it. Wanna feel you come," he growled.

His words were like an aphrodisiac. Each syllable strummed against my core as sure as his cock was filling me up. I moved faster. Lifting myself, and dropping back down, rocking into him, doing what my body wanted.

"That's it. Fuck. Look at your tits when you bounce around like that. S'good. You close, Angel?"

I nodded. I was.

Andres was filling me with so much heat, so much tactile sensation, I couldn't speak. Moving on instinct. I ran my hands over his shoulders, rubbing his biceps, his pecs, everywhere I could reach.

I just couldn't get enough. I had to spread my legs wider to get him where I needed him, but doing that meant I lost my purchase.

He was so big. So hard.

"I got you. Tell me how you want it," he grunted, hands squeezing my ass, thumb pressed against my puckered hole as he moved me up and down on his dick.

"Harder. Faster," I commanded.

One hand moved between us, and I felt him

sliding his fingers around the slickness we'd created, then he was back to grabbing my ass. The thumb at my back entrance was more persistent.

"Andres!" I moaned.

It felt good. Was it supposed to feel good?

"Push out, Lupina. That's it," he huffed, and I obeyed, moaning as his thumb slid into my ass.

"Oh fuck," I moaned, clamping my mouth over Andres' neck as the first wave of orgasmic bliss flooded my veins.

"Take it, take it!" Andres groaned, slamming his hips up, jiggling the thumb buried in my asshole, and pressing me down on his pulsating cock.

Heat speared me, wetness spilled down my thighs as his dick continued to spill inside of me.

"I love you," I said, clinging to Andres, knowing in my heart he loved me back, and feeling for the first time like I was exactly where I was supposed to be.

"I love you, Lupina. You were always mine," he said, and I smiled against his warm skin, believing every word.

"Happy Birthday, Nana!" Sammy yelled and helped my mother to blow out the candles on her cake.

I held my son up so he could reach them, but I looked at Ellie, catching the joy on her face as she snapped pictures. She smiled at me from her place next to Gabby, Mom's best friend, and the woman Ellie once thought I might be cheating on her with.

It wasn't funny at the time, but once Ellie saw the elderly woman with gray curls sitting in her wheelchair with a crocheted lap blanket spread across her, along with a dozen knitting projects, my wife had blushed adorably.

"Okay, does everyone have room for cake?" Mom

asked, and a round of deep masculine yeses went around the room.

I was surprised when Adrik, Marat, Josef, and their families had said yes after Ellie insisted that I invite them to Mom's birthday. It was the Saturday right after Thanksgiving, and I expected them to be tuckered out.

We'd spent half the holiday at Adrik's and Sofia's and the other half with Mom and her friends.

"Come help me cut the cake, Sammy!"

"Be careful," I said, letting my boy down to chase after his Nana.

I ambled over to Ellie, who smiled prettily at me, and held out my hand.

"You don't mind if I steal my wife, do you, Gabby?" I asked.

"Course not, Andres. But bring her back soon. We have crochet lessons to start next time I see her," the older woman said, winking at my wife.

Ellie blushed, her eyes going guiltily to the project Gabby was working on, and I frowned, trying to make heads or tails of what the woman was making.

"Is that a—"

"It is! I have my own store on Etsy now. Your mom helped me set it up, Andres. These are for a client who happens to be a romance author, she calls them *book boners*, isn't that cute?" the older woman laughed.

"*Book boners*? Ooh, let me see!" Sofia came running over.

I shook my head and tugged my wife closer to me.

"Crochet lessons, huh?"

She giggled and slid her arms around my neck.

"Well, I don't think I'll start with something quite as complicated as *book boners*, but maybe a baby blanket might be nice."

"Baby blanket?"

"Yeah, I thought. Well, when you're ready, maybe we can try," she started, but I was already crashing my mouth to hers.

Ellie moaned, kissing me back without reservation.

"Wanna get out of here?" I asked against her lips.

"Well, I suppose we can leave early. Sammy is looking forward to his sleep over with his Nana," my wife replied.

"**H**usband!" I cried out, scoring my nails down Andres' back.

The second I mentioned wanting to try for a baby, Andres went all caveman on me.

Not that I was complaining.

He picked me up when we were in the elevator, making my heart pound and my pulse race.

"I'm too heavy," I protested when he started to walk down the hall with me in his arms.

"Lupina," he tsked. "You don't think I can carry you to our bed?"

"Andres," I whined, biting my lip.

"You don't think I can hold you like this, and fuck you right here?" he asked, opening the condo door and backing me against the wall.

Moisture flooded between my legs, and I wiggled my hips, grateful for the long skirt I wore to his mother's party.

"Hold on," he growled.

"W-what?" I asked, distracted by the fact he was sucking my nipple through my blouse.

"Fuck. So hot. Take my dick out, Ellie."

I did.

"Now, pull your panties to the side."

I moaned. He was so strong. So damn sexy.

"That's it, Angel. You're so fucking wet, aren't you? So needy for my cock."

I was.

"Please," I begged.

Andres didn't make me wait. He slid in with no resistance, and we both groaned. He pounded into me, his hands digging into my skin.

"This sweet fucking ass is mine. All mine, Angel. Tell me."

"Yours. Oh my God, Andres, I'm close."

"That's right. I can hold you and fuck you against the wall like this, Make you come all over my cock. I'm the only one who can do this for you," he grunted.

"Yes," I hissed.

"I need you to understand, I fucking love this

body. Every dimple, every curve, every bounce, and wiggle. This body made my son. It's gonna make my daughter next. Now come."

He pumped his hips at a punishing pace, lifting me up and down with his fingers digging into my ass. I held on. Taking it. Taking him.

Then I let go.

"Andres!"

Andres carried me to our bathroom, placing me on the vanity seat with a gentle kiss on my head. He ran a bath for us.

We made love again inside the warm water, soaking the floor. That time, it was slow and deliberate. An after effect of my husband throwing away my birth control pills.

"Now we're going to practice making a family, right now," he said, kissing me so sweetly.

After we dried off, Andres led me to bed, wrapping around my body and pressing his face into the back of my head just breathing me in.

He made me feel so loved. So special and cherished. Moved me so much that I said so.

"You're my life, Lupina. I know you don't know or understand why or how, but you are. Accept it, trust it, know that I'd do anything to keep you safe and happy and with me."

He was right, I didn't understand it, but I knew this was where I belonged.

With him.

I thought love was supposed to be this gentle, sweet thing. But I was wrong.

Andres had his moments. We both did. Where tenderness won out and pure affection reigned supreme. But he would always be my wild attraction.

My untamed lover.

My biggest supporter.

My unwavering oak.

Andres was the love of my life. He didn't want to change me or control me. He just wanted me.

And I wanted him right back.

Him and this life he gave me. With friends, family, passion, and love, *so much love*.

Yes, I wanted it, and I was going to keep it.

"I love you, Andres."

"Love you too, Wife."

A few hours later, I felt Andres move. He rumbled something about forgetting his phone in his pants pocket, kissed my head, and walked to the bathroom.

"What the hell!"

My husband's screech had me hightailing it to the bathroom in all my jiggly naked glory to find him standing there baked with his discarded pants in one hand and one foot raised, a look of horror on his face.

The brown smear gave it away, and classy wife that I was, I fell down laughing.

"Awww, Rocky left you a present," I said between giggles.

"Oh, you think that's funny? Wait till I wash my foot, then we'll see what's funny," he threatened, already washing his foot in the sink with copious amounts of soap, after flushing the little gift Rocky left on his slacks down the toilet.

I saw the gleam of mischief in Andres' eyes and with a screech of my own I raced back to the safety of our bed.

Anticipation left me breathless as I waited for my husband. I knew Andres would never hurt me. But I couldn't wait to see what kind of punishment he came up with.

Something undoubtedly naughty. Arousal heightened my breathing and slick moisture gathered between my legs.

"You ready, Wife?"

"Always," I replied, grinning when he pulled the blanket off my waiting body.

His stormy gaze flashed with passion as he raked his eyes over my naked body. The desire I saw there matched mine, and as I opened my arms, welcoming him in, I saw nothing but love and acceptance, pride, and possession, and it was everything I always wanted.

Andres was everything I ever wanted.

He's all I'll ever need.

God, how I loved him.

Ten years later.

I sighed, biting my lip as I paced up and down the hospital room. I could not believe she threw me out.

Me! Ha!

Zaika moya was going to have a lot to make up for after this.

"Dad, you're going to wear out the floor," Michaela, my beautiful daughter said, rolling her eyes at me before looking back at her phone.

"Ad, can I get you something?" Marat offered, and I shook my head.

The whole family was there. I took a moment and just looked around the private waiting room. This was the whole Volkov Clan.

Sofia's Nonna sat in a corner with Andres' mother Nancy. They were oohing and aaahing over photos of little Julia's first steps. Andres' third daughter had been born just under a year ago, and she was now napping in her carriage while her mama was busy wrangling their other little ones.

Meredith and Josef were sitting with their brood, patiently reading stories to their four little redheaded angels.

Marat and Destiny were busy helping their twins with long division, a nightmare of a process I didn't relish having to go through again.

"Mom is going to be okay, right?" Michaela asked, and I held out my arm to my almost-teenaged daughter.

"Of course. Zaika moya is a warrior. And you take after her," I told my precious.

Ten years between siblings was a lot. I should know. Yes, I worried about my wife and the new baby she was currently bringing into the world, but I knew she would be great.

Everything that woman did was great.

I didn't deserve her. Looking at my family, at the Volkov wolves, Marat, Josef, and Andres, I knew we all felt the same.

None of us deserved our wives, or the precious children they gifted us with. But they were ours.

We protected what was ours.

I used to think money was the answer to everything. But I was wrong. So wrong.

It wasn't money. It was love.

Wild. Passionate. Messy. Obsessive. And everlasting.

"Mr. Volkov, your wife is asking for you," a nurse said.

My head turned, and I squeezed Michaela once before taking off down the hall.

I would do anything for my wife. Anything.

"Another girl!" Marat announced several minutes after Adrik had raced down the hall to his wife's room.

Applause and congratulations shook the rafters, and I grinned as my wife hugged me tightly.

"You lost the bet, pay up," I told Marat as he handed me a cigar.

"No way, I bet on him having a girl. You owe me."

"Nuh uh," I said, shaking my head.

"Are you guys still doing that stupid bet? I mean, look around you," Destiny said, shaking her head.

"She's right. I told you it was stupid. But if you're too cheap to pay up," I taunted my cousin, knowing he hated being called cheap.

"Here," he growled, tossing the half dollar coin at me.

"Wow. Where did you even find that?" Sammy asked, picking it up off the floor.

"I don't know. Somewhere," Marat replied with a careless shrug.

My phone beeped, and I looked down, my eyes going hard at what I read. I could hardly believe it. After a decade of searching.

That motherfucker.

"What is it?" Josef asked.

"You two up for a little ride?"

They nodded, and I kissed Ellie on the lips.

"We'll be back in a couple of hours. You okay here?"

"Yeah. No worries. It will be a few hours before we can see the baby. The kids are fine."

<hr>

"I almost forgot about this warehouse," Marat murmured absently as we neared the Lincoln Tunnel property still owned by Volkov Industries.

The place loomed ahead and as I waited for the

driver to pull up outside, I allowed old anger to fill my veins.

I wasn't the same person I was a decade ago. But that didn't mean I was less. If anything, my love for Ellie and my devotion to her and our children had only increased.

"So, who we got here?" Josef said, entering the place first.

"Boss," Eduardo dipped his chin at Josef, then Marat and me.

"It's him. No mistakes this time."

I nodded, cracking my neck and removing my coat and tie. I grabbed a metal pipe off a shelf and walked into the room where a man sat bound and gagged.

I canted my head to the side, aware of Josef and Marat standing next to me.

"He had a little work done," Josef said.

"Plastic surgery is good, but DNA doesn't lie," Marat added.

Rage filled me. This man had been responsible for hurting my wife. The ethical and moral lines he'd crossed were nothing compared to what I was about to do.

But I didn't have to think twice about it. This was for Ellie.

"You should have stayed in South America, Doctor," I said, then I lifted the pipe and swung.

Afterwards, we left Eduardo and a crew to clean up. Memories of that day in Central Park swarmed my brain.

I could have lost Ellie and Sammy that day. Thank fuck for the Volkov wolves. Without them. I didn't know what I would have done.

But now I knew that whenever any of *ours* was threatened, it wasn't just one wolf who went hunting.

It was all of us.

We were a pack.

And pack was family.

The end.

Did you enjoy this Andres and Ellie's story?
Please consider dropping a line or two in a review so other readers can enjoy it, too.

Want more Wild Billionaire Books?
Visit my website and grab all four today:

https://www.cdgorri.com/series/wild-billionaire-romance
Now available in paperback, hardcover, and with new discreet covers.
Thank you and happy reading!

del mare alla stella,
C.D. Gorri

P.S. Indie authors like me count on word of mouth to get my books seen, so if you have a blog or a social media account and you want to post about my books, be sure to include #cdgorribooks so I can see it and I will share to too. THANK YOU.

Merciful Lies by C.D. Gorri

Lies can be merciful. It just depends on the why.

Anna

I knew the second I saw him, my life would change forever. When my brother offers me as payment to Nico Fury, the king of the Vipers, how can I refuse? Tattooed, built, and tall, he was the only man I saw when I walked into the room. It was like he occupied all the available space, sitting on his throne of blood, sweat, and lies.

Nerves assailed me, but I owed my brother too much to let anything happen to him. One night. That was all. But it would leave me wrecked. Actions always had consequences. Six months later, my brother was killed by a rival organization, and now they were after me.

There was only one place I could go to keep my unborn baby safe. I just hoped the king would be merciful.

***

Nico

Perfect things didn't exist, at least not in my experience. But she was pretty close. I had her in my bed for one night, and I couldn't shake the memory. No, I wasn't meant to keep soft things like Anna Keller. My life belonged to my crew, and we were a vicious group. Hell, we weren't called Vipers for nothing. But she was different. She made me want, and I loved and hated her for it. Anna was light in a world of constant darkness. She was all warmth and beauty like no other. And I craved her like a drug.
Six months had passed since I took her in return for clearing her brother's debt to me, but that man attracted trouble like honey did flies. It wasn't long before I learned Sam Keller had gotten himself killed. Less than an hour later, Anna came back to me, on her knees, asking for sanctuary.
I knew the moment I saw the swell of her stomach she was carrying my baby. Anna thought coming here would protect her, but she was walking right into the Viper's nest. Before I was finished, my little runaway would be begging me for mercy.
Merciful Lies is the first in the contemporary

romance series of connected standalones, Jersey Bad Boys. This series features familiar tropes such as enemies to lovers, forced proximity, arranged marriages, secret babies, and contains some violence and explicit scenes.

Cherry on Top Tales
HIS pickle
her JAM
USA TODAY BESTSELLING AUTHOR
C.D. GORRI

<u>Contemporary Romance Books:</u>

<u>Cherry On Top Tales</u>

Her Yule His Log

His Carrot Her Muffin

Her Chocolate His Bar

His Pickle Her Jam

<u>Wild Billionaire Romance</u>

His Wild Obsession

His Wild Temptation

His Wild Seduction

His Wild Attraction

<u>Jersey Bad Boys</u>

Merciful Lies

Devious Lies

Pitiful Lies

***

<u>Paranormal Romance Books:</u>

<u>Macconwood Pack Novel Series:</u>

<u>Macconwood Pack Tales Series:</u>

The Falk Clan Tales:

The Bear Claw Tales:

The Barvale Clan Tales:

Barvale Holiday Tales:

Purely Paranormal Romance Books:

The Wardens of Terra:

The Maverick Pride Tales:

Dire Wolf Mates:

Wyvern Protection Unit:

Jersey Sure Shifters/EveL Worlds:

The Guardians of Chaos:

Twice Mated Tales

Hearts of Stone Series

Moongate Island Tales

Mated in Hope Falls

Speed Dating with the Denizens of the Underworld

Hungry Fur Love

Island Stripe Pride

NYC Shifter Tales

A Howlin' Good Fairytale Retelling

Witch Shifter Clan

Young Adult/Urban Fantasy Books

The Grazi Kelly Novel Series

<u>The Angela Tanner Files</u>

<u>G'Witches Magical Mysteries Series</u>

Co-written with P. Mattern

<u>Witches of Westwood Academy</u>

with Gina Kincade

<u>Blackthorn Academy For Supernaturals</u>

*<u>*Be sure to check out my BUY DIRECT BUNDLES</u> and get 30% off when you buy available only my website.*

Click here for The Official C.D. Gorri Reading List - free download

Coming Soon

Motley Crewd Shifters

ABOUT THE AUTHOR

USA Today Bestselling author C.D. Gorri writes paranormal and contemporary romance and urban fantasy books with plenty of steam and humor.

Join her mailing list here: https://www.cdgorri.com/ newsletter

An avid reader with a profound love for books and literature, she is usually found with a book in hand. C.D. lives in her home state, New Jersey, where many of her characters and stories are based. Her tales are fast-paced yet detailed with satisfying conclusions. If you enjoy powerful heroines and loyal heroes who face relatable problems in supernatural settings, journey into the Grazi Kelly Universe today.

You will find sassy, curvy heroines and sexy, love-driven heroes who find their HEAs between the pages.

Wolves, Bears, Dragons, Tigers, Witches, Vampires, and tons more Shifters and supernatural creatures dwell within her paranormal works. The most important thing is every mate in this universe is fated, loyal, and true lovers always get their happily-ever-afters.

In her contemporary works, you will find fiercely possessive men and the smart, confident, curvy women they are crazy about. As always, the HEA is between the pages.

Thank you and happy reading!
del mare alla stella,
C.D. Gorri

http://www.cdgorri.com
https://www.facebook.com/Cdgorribooks
https://www.bookbub.com/authors/c-d-gorri
https://twitter.com/cgor22
https://instagram.com/cdgorri/
https://www.goodreads.com/cdgorri
https://www.tiktok.com/@cdgorriauthor

www.ingramcontent.com/pod-product-compliance
Lightning Source LLC
Chambersburg PA
CBHW022259310726
48973CB00001B/132